AN IRREGULAR PIECE OF SKY
AND OTHER STORIES

Other Books by Ian Gouge

Novels and Novellas

Tilt - Coverstory books, 2023
Once Significant Others - Coverstory books, 2023
On Parliament Hill - Coverstory books, 2021
A Pattern of Sorts - Coverstory books, 2020
The Opposite of Remembering - Coverstory books, 2020
At Maunston Quay - Coverstory books, 2019
An Infinity of Mirrors - Coverstory books, 2018 (2nd ed.)
The Big Frog Theory - Coverstory books, 2018 (2nd ed.)
Losing Moby Dick and Other Stories - Coverstory books, 2017

Short Stories

An Irregular Piece of Sky - Coverstory books, 2023
Degrees of Separation - Coverstory books, 2018
Secrets & Wisdom - Paperback, 2017

Poetry

Crash - Coverstory books, 2023
not the Sonnets - Coverstory books, 2023
Selected Poems: 1976-2022 - Coverstory books, 2022
The Homelessness of a Child - Coverstory books, 2021
The Myths of Native Trees - Coverstory books, 2020
First-time Visions of Earth from Space - Coverstory books, 2019
After the Rehearsals - Coverstory books, 2018
Punctuations from History - Coverstory books, 2018
Human Archaeology - Paperback, 2017
Collected Poems (1979-2016) - KDP, 2017

Non-Fiction

Shrapnel from a Writing Life - Coverstory books, 2022

IAN GOUGE

AN IRREGULAR PIECE OF SKY
AND OTHER STORIES

First published in paperback format by
Coverstory books, 2023

ISBN 978-1-7393569-6-5 (Paperback)
ISBN 978-1-7393569-7-2 (eBook)

www.iangouge.com

www.coverstorybooks.com

Contents

The Seeds of Poppies 3
Park'n'Ride 51
Damage 55
Downsizing 69
Smoking in the Park 73
The Big Red Button 87
Hope 103
Ursula 119
After All This Time 125
Out of the Woods 145
Through a Glass Darkly 153
Extra-curricular 171
Steak 183
Blue 187
An Irregular Piece Of Sky 193

❋

Acknowledgements...207

The Seeds of Poppies

He is lost as soon as he drops the stone into the water. Lost to his childhood, thirty years evaporating just like that.

Downstream from the waterfall, where it is quieter, the river fragments somewhat, flexing to fit in with the geology of the place, lacking the will to do anything other than pursue the path of least resistance. Stepping across boulders that edged the main body of the river, he had discovered a small parallel spur running in isolation for a few yards and then gathering into a modest reservoir before leaking back to the parent flow. The shallow rivulet is no more than eight inches wide just above the pool, and it is here he pauses, mesmerised by the water's surface as it jostles against stone. The loose rock, almost cuboid and about three inches wide, had been disturbed by his left foot. His bending to retrieve it was instinctive, yet his placing of it just where the pool began to be formed is more deliberate than not, stimulated by a desire to see how locating it there might affect the skin of water now forced to take a modified route. The resulting new eddies in the basin further captivate him, and for a moment he is transported to another place, back to another time.

Building a dam is the only possible next step. A common enough activity for young children, his memories take him back to Devon and the house they had lived in for those three magical years, and to the stream that ran through the woods beyond the end of their garden. He had been six or seven, Josh three years older, and together they had tried again and again to create a sticks-and-stones structure which would hold back the water; every time they succeeded in interrupting the flow, the shape of it, but always failed to achieve their signal goal. Between them, age-wise, Bernie sat in her favourite spot on the opposite bank, a little withdrawn, partly on their mother's instruction and partly because she did not trust the tranquility of something that could shift so subtly, whose essence was invisible. It had been during those summers he first learned of the power of water and its fascination for him; years later Josh would tell him how he too had learned how precious it was, but that in his case he'd needed to be lost in a desert to be granted such knowledge. Looking around, he finds more loose stones of various sizes and assembles a collection, settling them on the boulder that separates his pool from the main stream. Then, crouching down as he had decades ago, he goes to work, a builder once again trying to exercise some kind of supremacy over the natural world.

Having placed two more stones, he looks up, half-expecting to see a figure watching from the far bank. Perpetually unsettled by her, back then he would often pause in his endeavours and look across the brook to where she sat.

"Will you write about this, Bernie?" he asked.

"Of course," she said with a strange certainty that belied her age. "I write about everything."

And she had. While he and Josh tried more and more elaborate devices to dam the water, Bernie - christened Bernadette but hating the length and complexity of the word - sat and watched, occasionally scribbling in her plain-covered notebook. At the point when they instinctively knew they were done, he and Josh would stand up only to realise she was no longer there, as if she had seen the end coming, almost foretold it. Back at the house, their socks and shoes inevitably drenched, Bernie would most likely be sitting at the kitchen table drinking lemonade or eating a biscuit, watching their mother as she prepared a meal, or cleaned, or unloaded their rudimentary washing machine. She would write about all of that too. It had been disconcerting when, years later, he had first read her fictionalised versions of them all, captured in black-and-white and immortalised between hardback covers as if they had been trapped in amber like prehistoric insects.

He looks down at this modern incarnation and his solo efforts thus far. There is more of a whirl on the surface now, the water having to climb over his recently placed stones before angling down into the pool via a narrower channel. It is different, but nothing like a dam. He thinks about stopping or taking a video with his phone but does neither. Bending once again to be close to the water, he lifts another small rock, trying to decide where it should go.

Their Devon idyll was brought to an end by a combination of death and sickness. The heart attack that claimed his paternal grandfather had taken them all by surprise, and although the children loved him in the way grandchildren are supposed to, they never really knew him as a person. Perhaps that is most often the way. Always preferring the practical, when the news came his father took stock of the situation and organised his troops accordingly. They would have to move. His own mother - the children's 'best granny' - had been suffering with dementia for some time, and with her husband and primary carer now departed, the depth of her own illness was exposed to the rest of the family for the first time.

"The house is plenty big enough," he remembered his father explaining, "after all, I grew up there with *my* brothers and sisters! So you'll each have your own room - probably bigger than your bedroom here - and there's a huge garden and an orchard." He tried to make it sound like a landed estate.

"But we'll have to change schools," Josh had protested.

"I know, son; but it can't be helped. Granny needs us."

He and Josh had exchanged glances.

"But what about the river?" he asked.

"The river!" Both his parents laughed, assuming it was a joke. "I'm afraid we can't take it with us, Dobs."

"I know that," he said, then paused. "But is there a river at Granny's house?"

His mother had walked to where he sat, the five of them round the kitchen table in a council of war.

"You know what granny's house is like," she said softly. "There isn't a river near her garden like the one here. But I'm sure there must be one not so very far away. Isn't that so?" She glanced at her husband who failed to reply.

After the meeting was over - the children's reward for their attention being an ice-pop from the freezer - he and Josh went out into the garden to play and talk about the future. They agreed saying goodbye to the river would be hard. Bernie went up to her room and opened a notebook.

Based on a short holiday in the New Forest when he had been five, he had declared a passion for horses; he would, he announced, be a jockey or a vet or the most famous racehorse trainer in the world. Inevitably he had become none of those things. Josh had immediately christened him Dobbin, a name which - once it had been inadvertently adopted by his parents - became shortened to Dobs. And Dobs had stuck. They had chosen to christen him Jonathan, but as a child it was a name he never liked nor grew into. As he got older, his parents tried to move away from his childhood nickname, rotating through all the usual derivatives of Jonathan to see if any of them resonated. None did. Consequently they only tended to be used - Jon, Jonny or Jonathan itself - whenever he had done something wrong or was in trouble; and eventually the family stopped calling on them at all. Bowing to the inevitable, as a fast-maturing teenager he started introducing himself to new acquaintances as "Jonathan Wells, though my friends call me

Dobs". It had been a deliberate perpetuation he thought made him interesting, though one he was forced to abandon as soon as he started to earn a living, realising that 'Dobs' lacked professional credibility. Beginning with Jon, as his roles increased in seniority so he began to use longer versions of his name. If you walked up to him now, nearly twenty years later, bent over the water with a stone in each hand, he would introduce himself as Jonathan - and do so in a tone suggesting that something had come full circle.

Names had never been an issue for Josh. Devoid of a nickname - he was always Josh or Joshua - he joked that the Army gave him new ones anyway. When he entered Afghanistan he had been Lieutenant Wells; Captain Wells when he left. Later, once he had been demobbed, he came to think of those regimental names as being more statements of geography than anything else. Returning to his academic roots and his first love of forestry management, a few years later - walking through acres of pines in Northumberland - he told Jonathan that those appellations "belonged to a different place and a different person".

"Don't you think about the war?" his brother had asked him.

Josh had paused and looked up.

"I only think about trees," he said, the soft accompaniment of their feet on pine needles closing the conversation.

Placing the stones in the water, Jonathan remembers that walk and the silence which followed it. In a strange way it had been the most eloquent Josh had ever been with him. Looking down, he wonders what that nine-year-old version of his brother would have done with the few rocks that remained. The first one he had set down had already been submerged as the water, persistent and undeniable, found new ways to reach its goal. He had changed the shape of it - and in places the pace of the flow - but that was all. He smiled to himself. It was that old lesson again; the one about invincibility and destiny.

Bernie always maintained her own destiny had been set from the start and that she had never deviated from it. Hers was a drive softened thanks to a blend of determination and compassion, present even when she was too young to really know what was actually going on. By the time he was nine, Jonathan had stopped asking "will you write about this, Bernie?" because she wrote about everything; the good and the bad, the sad and the happy. Once, when he was studying for his O-levels and struggling with Shakespeare, she had informed him that the only thing writers were trying to do - Shakespeare included - was to make sense of the world, and it was simply that some people were better at it than others.

"Better at making sense of the world?" Jonathan had sought to qualify.

Bernie laughed.

"No; writing, silly! No-one can really make sense of the world."

It had been a correction delivered without malice or meanness, and - given how often she fell to correcting him at that time - he assumed with a kindness that must have been a constant challenge for her. Only later did he realise it was just another manifestation of how she was made, someone whose mission was to help others see what was right before their eyes.

Standing upright once again, he feels a slight twinge in his back, his right arm finding the guilty spot as if doing so will resolve the issue. "It's just age," he tells himself. The question about what to do next, whether or not to carry on, is simultaneously answered, and he looks down at the remapped rivulet and wonders if he has made any difference. It is a question which - in its most wide-ranging sense - has come to haunt him more and more. Even though he doesn't talk about it, Jonathan assumes Josh made a difference of some kind during the war in Afghanistan. And he knows Bernie has. Casting another glance across to the far bank, he hears her voice as it came to him through the telephone.

"I wanted you to know from me," she had said.

"Know what?"

"About the book. That I've written about you."

He laughed.

"You were always writing about me, about us."

"But now there's a book, Dobs. A proper book. A cover, a publisher and everything."

How old had they been? Early thirties?

"And I'm in it?"

"Yes and no." She paused. "It's a fiction, of course, but part of it is based on our time in Devon when we were children. And there are characters in it that look a little bit like us. You, me, Josh." She paused again. "I wanted you to know, for you to not be surprised. In case you ever read it."

Bernie had never let them read anything she wrote; even her essays from school she kept distanced from her parents. It was as if she had a store of treasure she was intent on building up and keeping secret. He recalls once seeing a pile of notebooks on her bed before she ushered him out of the room.

"So I *am* in it?"

She laughed.

"Only bits of you."

"I hope the good bits," he joked. She said nothing. "What's it called, this book of yours?"

"'The Seeds of Poppies' by Bernadette Wells."

"'Bernadette'?"

"My publisher said I needed to use my proper name for it to be clear that I was a woman. 'Bernie' clouded the issue, he said. And anyway, we each have them don't we?"

"What, issues?"

"No." He could tell from her laugh that she was perhaps as happy as she had ever been. "Our professional names: Captain, Jonathan, Bernadette. See?"

"Okay." As much as he had longed to, what she had just said felt like a stone he was instantly disinclined to turn over. "And what's it about, 'The Seeds of Poppies'?"

"Oh, about how people are always not the same people they once were…"

Was that true? He walks away from the great slabs of rock that corralled the river, the memory of her words echoing in his head. It seemed a little disingenuous to question whether Bernie was correct, that they had indeed become different people. One of the few truisms in his life was that ninety-nine times out of a hundred Bernie was right. For example, how many times had Josh changed from the brother with whom he had built dams in Devon? When he went to college? When he went to war? And again when he came back? Jonathan wonders what Josh would have been like if he had not enlisted, or had not been sent to the desert. Would he still be living his hermit life in Northumberland, a loner communing with trees? And what about himself?

As he reaches the path proper and heads back up the side of the valley towards his parked car, he realises he doesn't want to think about the Jonathan Wells he has become; so instead he tries to focus on Bernie, the sister who seemed to have gone from being a no-one to a someone overnight - at least as far as the rest of the world was concerned. The book had been well received. It had been picked up and promoted heavily by Waterstones in the UK and Barnes and Noble in the States, her publisher doing his job exceptionally well. Sales exceeded expectations; it was nominated for an award; they issued a paperback with a modified cover, the words "One of the best debut novels in a generation" emblazoned on it. Sales spiked again. There were rumours about The Booker though these never materialised into anything concrete. She sent him a copy with two kisses drawn beneath her name on the title page - her equivalent of a signature. He had been astonished by her work, enthralled, seeing elements of the three of them in the characters she had drawn, portrayals so perceptive that at times she had made him want to cry.

"Tell me," the interviewer had asked during her first public exposure, a small slot on a Radio 4 book programme, "the title. Why 'The Seeds of Poppies'? It's not about the First World War, after all."

"No, it isn't." Jonathan had recognised the slight catch in her voice, the tell that said she was needing to be patient; patient and kind. It was a tone he had heard often enough. "But isn't it true that the devastation, turmoil and carnage of the First World War surfaced poppy seeds that had long been dormant, and that a year or two later they had flowered, were suddenly everywhere? Well I believe people are like that. That we each of us have a myriad of seeds within us that are waiting to be awoken, and once they are they flower and things change."

"But not because of war?"

"Of course not. It could be anything. The simplest of things - or the grandest and most complex. A smile; playing by a river; seeing a bird in the sky. Or a birth or death, a wedding or divorce. Anything. And at any time. Or all the time. And each of the things we do or say, that we see or hear, that is said to us or done to us, releases one or more of these little dormant seeds, changes who we are, what we do next, what people see, how they feel about us. And how we feel about ourselves."

"Nature or nurture?" the interviewer had asked, trying too hard to sound intellectual.

"I don't know," Bernie had said, somewhat flatly, "you tell me. I believe that when we are born we could achieve anything, be anything, and what we eventually become depends on which of those little seeds germinate. And which do not. Sometimes we do things or don't do things or have things done to us that means some seeds will lie dormant. Forever."

Jonathan had assumed that during their time in Devon the three of them had been planting rather than harvesting, but he now knew Bernie was right. He pauses to look back down the path to where, out of sight, the river flowed. He had been drawn to the water, compelled to try and build a dam once again, not because the seed had been planted in Devon, but because already present, there it had germinated.

Thinking of Devon, he recalls seeing Josh a few months after Bernie's book had been published.

"You've read it?" he asked his brother.

"I have not," Josh said, slipping into the vaguely military tone he tended to adopt when he wanted to avoid the emotional.

"Why not? It's truly wonderful - and I'm not saying that because Bernie's our sister."

"I'm sure it is." He had paused for a moment. "You know, Dobs," it sounded like the beginning of a confession, "I've never doubted her. Never. I've always thought that there was something special about her, that she had been touched by something the likes of you and I could only dream of. A gift perhaps. Stardust. All that writing. All that seriousness. It was never going to be for nothing, not for Bernie."

"So will you read it?"

"I will not."

"Why not?"

"Because Mum hated it." He waited long enough for silence to fill the gap between them. "She read it as soon as it was out, of course; and of course she's as proud as it's possible for a mother to be. And I'm proud of Bernie too. And humbled, in a way. But Mum felt the book was some kind of betrayal; of the life we led back then, of us as individuals. I think she saw it as a criticism of her. Even though she knew it was a story, she could see too many things in Bernie's characters that reminded her of us and exposed what we were like and what we did - and in her reading, through her lens, too little of that was positive. For her it was a critique that wasn't fiction at all."

It had perhaps been the longest speech Josh had ever made - except when Jonathan had forced him to be Best Man at both his weddings.

"Really?" Jonathan tried to recall the relevant sections of the book. Josh waited. "Maybe I can see where she's coming from - but you'd have to want to read it in that way... I guess once the idea's in your head you're stuck with it." Was that all he needed to say? "But that's not the book I read; not my interpretation of it. Not at all."

Josh nodded almost imperceptibly. Message received.

"You don't want to make up your own mind?"

Josh shook his head.

"I'm just happy being happy for Bernie. And unbelievably proud of her. Please don't assume I'm not. But I have no desire to find out if Mum's right or wrong. That would abandon me in no-man's-land, either way. So I'm going to leave it where it is. You tell me it's brilliant, Dobs, and I believe you because I trust your judgement. You know more about these sorts of things than I do. And to be honest, you telling me that confirms an assumption I'd already made."

So there they all were, Jonathan thought, the four of them perpetually linked through Bernie's book. One way or another. All that writing, all those notebooks; she had made use of the material they had collectively gifted her just by being and doing. And now, whether she'd intended to or not, she had held up a mirror of sorts to them all. As he reaches his car, he finds he is still unable to reconcile his mother's view with his own, a gulf seeming to exist between their two positions. Ever since his conversation with Josh he has wanted to ask her about it, to hear it from her own lips, but he has deliberately avoided the subject, not wishing to upset her. He would have to defend his position, the book, Bernie too perhaps, and that might end up serving no positive purpose whatsoever. Josh's stance is understandable.

He pauses before starting the car. He wonders what his father would have made of 'The Seeds of Poppies', whether his view would have aligned with their mother's or his own. Treacherous or brilliant? Or both, perhaps. But of course this is a question that cannot be asked, a conversation that cannot be had. Having died nearly five years ago now, Jonathan still wonders who misses him most, knowing it is not him. It would be easy to assume that it was his mother, but he isn't sure. Perhaps it is Josh, as their father had been instrumental in steering his eldest son toward The Army. Perhaps Bernie - or then again maybe least of all Bernie. Had their father's death actually freed her to undertake the book? Would it have been impossible for her to write - never mind publish - if he had still been alive? It was not beyond the realms of possibility that the reason their mother had so taken against it was that she regarded 'The Seeds of Poppies' as a posthumous attack on him - even though it wasn't. Maybe his mother had adopted anger on his behalf. "People are always not the same people they once were" Bernie had said; and even though her characters were fictional, perhaps she was challenging them all - herself included - to say "look at what we were - and what we have become".

Had it been posed as a direct question, of all of them Josh would surely have been best placed to answer. Perhaps that was why he never talked about his experience in The Army because it had forced him to be someone different, someone else. And only he could know if what he had become - solitary and so resolutely independent - had been as a result of Afghanistan or as a defence mechanism, a kind of self-protection. He confessed himself 'content' with his life, though Jonathan struggled to align the word's meaning with what he saw. As he pulls out from the car park and onto the road, he wonders if Bernie has seen him since the book had come out. Indeed, when had she seen him last - sequestered in his forested world - and had she written about it? Jonathan smiles. The second part of that particular question is entirely superfluous of course. Then it strikes him that perhaps Josh was being economical with the truth when it came to his reason for not wanting to read her book. Might it have been that he didn't want to recognise in those old selves the person he had once been? Such a reminder would surely have brought into even stronger relief how much he had changed. As such, it was most likely a recollection to be avoided at all costs.

*

"So how are you?" She tries to find a tone of light-hearted concern, even though it does not come naturally to her.

"Checking up on me?" he asks in reply, the monotone flatness of his voice exaggerated by the phone and by her not being able to see him.

She is momentarily annoyed that he sounds so disinterested.

"Aren't I allowed to check-in on my big brother?"

The lockdown had begun two weeks earlier. The streets and roads were deserted which only enhanced the sense that a plague had descended upon them all.

"I may be taller than you, but strictly speaking I'm not your big brother."

"I know that," she says, "but if there's one person who's going to be okay at the moment it's Josh; he was already in his own kind of lockdown. I doubt he'll have noticed the difference."

"Don't you think that's a tad unfair?"

"Probably," she feigns to agree, even though she doesn't. She knows both her brothers will be alone right now, the difference being that Jonathan has never quite been able to come to terms with it, whereas for Josh it's simply the status quo. And all the while he has his trees he won't really be alone. "Can you work from home?"

"Just about, I suppose." There is resignation in his voice. "All the meetings are virtual of course, phone and video; I don't think I've ever spent so much time on my computer. But it has it's benefits."

"Such as?"

"Oh, when I need to I can concentrate on things, if I need to write a report or something, or prepare a presentation."

She tries to process the notion of giving a presentation without a real audience, then gives up both preparation and performance as pointless exercises.

"And who are you spending lockdown with?"

It is a question she was not expecting, as if he shouldn't have needed to ask it.

"No-one of course. Why?"

"No reason. I just wondered if Guy was holed-up with you."

She can't imagine being 'holed-up' at all, never mind with Guy. It is one of the blessings with what she does: she can be anywhere she chooses to be.

"That," she says, trying to inject a little humour into the conversation, "would require something of a change in the status of our relationship which, although Guy might be keen to explore it, I most certainly am not. No, like everyone else my lockdown is punctuated by glimpses of the postman, distanced conversations with delivery drivers, and faces in little Zoom squares."

"Indeed." He pauses, she waits. "Are you writing?" When she can't help but laugh, she finds herself hoping it is not in any way a cruel laugh. "Silly question, I know."

"No, not silly at all." She tries to sound reassuring. "In fact it's a very good question - though it should be prefixed with 'what'." Has that done the trick? "My publisher is keen for me to be working on a follow-up to 'Poppies' to prove I'm not a 'one-hit-wonder'. He says the second book is always the hardest."

"And is it? I mean, is he right do you think?"

"Not really. Well, not in my case anyway."

"That's good then, isn't it?" There is something in his voice that suggests he is struggling to keep up his side of the conversation. "What's it about?"

"I don't think I can say just yet - not because I don't want to, but because I haven't settled on anything totally final."

If it is a lie - even a partial one - she can tell it has been delivered successfully, a brief silence suggesting he wants to change the subject of the conversation. She senses - partly because Dobs is her brother but also because she has a knack for such things - that what he wants to talk about most of all is himself, the silence carrying the weight of his loneliness.

"Have you spoken to Mum?" He beats her to the draw.

"Have you?" It is another way of saying 'no', though she is sure he will not pick up on it, preferring to accept the literal.

"A couple of days ago. She seems fine. As you say, it's all posties and the man who drives the Tesco van - though I think in her case she also has a group of friends who seem to be supporting each other; you know, phone calls, conversations over garden fences. It sounds like they're being a little renegade at times."

The use of the word 'renegade' impresses her. It is, she realises on hearing it, a wonderful word and one she must use.

He carries on.

"And I've spoken to Josh too. He is, as you say, pretty much unaffected, unfazed. Probably just about 'un' anything."

She laughs, briefly.

"What was the last interesting thing you did before we were all confined to barracks, Dobs? Tell me." The mention of Josh subconsciously informs her simile. She makes a mental note of that too.

"Me? Nothing too dramatic." There is a short hiatus; 'thinking time'. "A walk probably. Not too far from here there's a waterfall. Have I ever taken you there? Nothing too grand or dramatic - we don't do grand or dramatic do we? - but pleasant enough." Bernie wonders who he means by 'we'. "It was funny. I went down to the water's edge. There was a little part of the stream that had broken away - just a tiny sliver really - and I found myself trying to build a dam with stones and things."

"A dam?"

"I know!" He picks up on the note of surprise in her voice, though misinterprets the reason for it being there. "Just like we did in Devon when we were kids - though the location and circumstances were obviously different. But that's what I did. It made me think about us."

"Us?"

"You know; you, me, Josh. How we were when we were younger, you writing everything down. And then your book and how wonderful it was. Stuff like that."

Knowing he is expecting a response, some kind of affirmation, she takes her time. It seems strange it should take an event like that for him to think about important things when she feels as if she is doing so all the time. In a way, such a walk would have been interesting for her only if it had allowed her *not* to think, or analyse, or dissect.

"That does sound fun. And were there any conclusions?"

"Conclusions?"

"To your thinking; what you thought about. Were you struck by a flash of inspiration or enlightenment? Was anything suddenly clear?"

"Clear? Not really. In fact there just seemed to be more questions to be answered. Or rather questions for me to answer, I suppose. Nothing earth-shattering, just 'life stuff'."

Later she thinks about the nature of questions. It was typical of Dobs that he should be either inventing or uncovering them. As far as she could see, his life had been ruled by uncertainty; there was always something he didn't know or didn't understand. Was it any wonder that both his marriages had failed, corrupted by his indecisiveness? He and Bernie were opposites, of course: where he raised queries, she saw her mission to provide answers - even to questions that had yet to be asked. She liked to think that she observed, rarely questioned. What was the point? The sky was blue, the sun shone, people married, divorced, loved, betrayed, died. She could do nothing about any of that. So she had chosen to interpret and to replay, to offer lenses through which people could look and maybe glimpse answers to some of their own questions.

Was that right, though? Had she 'chosen' to undertake that role? Actually it didn't matter. Just another irrelevant question. The fact is that is who she is and that's what she's doing; it is her purpose. She has no other. To that extent she is 'sorted' in a way that Jonathan could never be - though in turn she suspects she might never be as resolved as Josh. Not only did he no longer ask questions, he didn't feel the need to seek answers either. She recalls an earlier conversation with him. It had been brief and dissatisfying, almost as if they had been speaking a different language; there had been no connection, two people who had inadvertently collided for the briefest of moments, arriving from parallel universes, worlds where how things worked were the antithesis of each other. In his case she had no doubt almost everything he was or thought or felt could be explained by his experiences in the war in Afghanistan. Josh's PTSD had manifested itself in a definite way, driving him into the protective shell of his hermit-like existence, taking as companions the silent trees which surrounded and protected him. He has no need of either questions or answers, and because of that she suspects he would hate *Poppies* and the people in it - not just because the family were all there to some extent, but because in Josh's eyes her characters would be too weak, too fallible, too needy. Yet wasn't that how the vast majority of people were?

An image of Guy pops into her head, though she has no clear idea of the word which has provided the bridge between he and Josh. They are 'chalk and cheese' - though to be fair that could be said about Josh in comparison with just about anyone. Guy remains as he has always been: tall, professional, charming. He is polite, dresses well (but is not too showy), is considerate, attentive, respected. Perhaps what speaks the most - or the least - for him is the fact that her mother had been bowled over by him the first time they had met, he and Bernie on a flying visit to the West Country and dropping in to see her at her retreat on the edge of the Quantocks. In many respects Guy's constancy is the exception which proves Bernie's rule that everyone is always changing; he is now, quite simply, almost entirely as he had been when she met him. Perhaps that had been part of his attraction. Their father had just died and Bernie had settled on the theme, plot and structure of her book. Knowing there would be dark writing days ahead, she had wanted companionship of some kind, a shoulder to cry on; but simultaneously, she needed to avoid unnecessary distraction. Guy had offered her all of that, her judgement of him as accurate as it tended to be about most people. With a twinge of guilt, the word she most now associates with him is 'adequate'. Yet from their earlier time together she'd had no complaints. And though he appears not to have changed at all in the last three years, she sees subtleties beneath the surface that other people would miss, shifts in his attitude towards her that only materialise when they are alone.

Whether it is due to the passage of time or - if she is being cruel - the impact of her 'arrival' on the literary scene and all that might imply, Guy has become increasingly serious about their relationship. The word he now uses with more noticeable regularity - 'us' - portends to a future in which she has little interest. *Poppies* has not only changed her life, but inevitably - and not ironically! - changed her too. If she is honest with herself, she feels the need to move beyond 'adequate'. And Guy is not the man for that particular job.

What to do next as far as he is concerned is a conundrum she would like to share with someone else, to debate, to chase ideas down rabbit holes before abandoning them; but she knows none of the candidates at her disposal are up to the task. Jonathan wouldn't have the capacity - intellectual or emotional - to keep up with her; and Josh either wouldn't understand or wouldn't care. Possibly both. Her mother disqualifies herself on the basis that she would undoubtedly bat on Guy's behalf and be entirely happy for Bernie to settle for 'adequate' - not that she settled for average herself, at least not in the early days. Perhaps having children changed her perspective. All their father's rough edges had been sanded down by the time the three of them were old enough to get to know him, but even then Bernie caught glimpses of the man he'd once been - bold, adventurous, challenging. That earlier version - had she been able to tap into it - would certainly have provided her with a viable option for a confidant, if only he hadn't managed to get himself riddled with the cancer that had been quietly growing inside him, a legacy from his youth as a heavy smoker and general 'bon viveur'. Perhaps it had been his marginal encroachment on a life of 'sex, drugs and rock-and-roll' that had seduced her mother back in the day. Bernie had included hints of that mythological man in one of her book's main characters - probably one of the reasons she was sure her mother had taken against it.

Having drawn a blank in terms of sounding-board candidates available to her - and having no suitable close friends, male or female - Bernie has chosen to invent one. She has begun a fictional dialogue into which she has inserted herself alongside a gender-neutral 'Pat' to see if they can work out what she is going to do about Guy. Pat has two major advantages: their opinion is not clouded by an overlay of sex, and they know Guy as well as Bernie does. Indeed, Bernie wonders if it might just prove that they know *her* better than she does herself. The motion to be debated is a more complex question than simply deciding on how to remove Guy from the picture; she needs to know whether she is going to replace him, and if so, what - in the broadest sense - she should be looking for. With her new best friend already displaying an acute understanding of the dilemma faced - their debut pronouncement unequivocally stating that Guy's departure must be the first priority - Bernie has growing confidence that Pat will help her find a solution.

*

- 'Moving on'. That's so crass and common; I apologise for burdening you with it.

- There's no need to apologise, B; really. And remember, you can make me say whatever you want to… But you're right.

- I'm 'white'?!

- Now who's playing games!

- Shall we get back to the task in hand?

- Now that you've surgically removed Guy the Gorilla from the scene.

- Isn't that a little unkind, Pat?

- Not at all, B. Guy the Gorilla was a well-loved inmate of London zoo for many years. The star attraction, perhaps.

- And you're drawing a parallel how, exactly?

- You misunderstand me. Or yourself.

- Hmmm. But was Guy's 'removal' - as you call it - particularly 'surgical'? The man, not the gorilla. I thought I let him down gently enough.

- You could be right; don't forget, you're the wordsmith here... Perhaps I would have said 'efficient' rather than 'surgical'. Or 'economical'. It was quick and decisive. I would also like to think there was some kindness in your approach. Even so, afterwards he could have had no doubt it was all over, could he?

- That was the intention, Pat.

- So, mission accomplished then.

- Now it's all about what next.

- And you're sure there has to be a next?

- What do you mean?

- Couldn't you could take some 'time out' (my turn to be vulgar!), treat yourself to some semi-splendid isolation. Remove all external distractions while you focus on book number two.

- I'm not my brother, Pat.

- Which one? Because from certain perspectives, they both qualify.

- I was thinking of Josh.

- The obvious one. Of course there's a story there; I mean, all alone in his dark forest, completely uninterested in any meaningful interactions with the outside world.

- I'm not sure that's fair.

- You said it, kiddo.

- You forget what he's been through.

- *I* forget what he's been through?! Why are you laughing, B?

- This feels like our first row. Interesting.

- Isn't it?

- Anyway, what about Jonathan. From whose perspective does he 'qualify'?

- Yours, B. And the fact that he is, in his own way, just as isolated as Josh. Two failed relationships - at least -

- That's unfair.

- Perhaps; but not necessarily untrue. So two failed relationships; drifting along somewhat aimlessly. An uninspiring sort of life. Not that's what I'm advocating for you, of course. Just painting a picture. Drawing a thread.

- A thread?

- She always had a soft spot for you, you know.

- Who did?

- Dobs' wife.

- Greta?

- The scourge of Europe? Don't be daft! No, Pammy; his first failure.

- No-one called her Pammy.

- Well not yet anyway. Doesn't she still send you cards at Christmas and for your birthday.

- So what?

- So I was wondering if a little 'exploration' might be on the cards. A dalliance, if you like - purely for research purposes.

- You're not suggesting…

- If I were you I wouldn't completely buy into Jonathan's narrative about why they broke up. Two sides to every story and all that. And just ask yourself, why hasn't she shacked-up with some other bloke in the last, few years? Nothing serious. Or long-term. Maybe nothing at all.

- You don't mean?

- I'm just saying, B. *You're* the one who does all the 'meaning'…

❊

A year on and it had been an unusual winter in terms of the weather. Still not totally cleansed of the monotony of the desert, Josh has rediscovered his seasonal routine is dependant on the timely appearance of sun, rain and snow - though, thanks to the pandemic turmoil, at least the general absence of visitors has provided him with a little flexibility. Not that were ever that many visitors anyway. As part of his responsibilities for the various swathes of forest for which he has oversight, he keeps the signs promoting the entries into their car parks in excellent condition, everything distinct and legible; yet it seems to make little difference. Whilst the repeated lockdowns have not helped numbers, he also believes that many 'natural' tourist sights such as his fall into the 'nice idea' category; the kinds of place where, when people drive past, they say "we must go there!" but never do. Only the regular few turn up; the committed and the passionate. The fact that he has not been feeling particularly well for a few days now he also attributes to the weather. After the heat and sun of the desert, he relishes the cold, and embraces brilliantly crisp and clear mornings: hard frost on the ground; the trees dusted in white ice crystals; a last glorious winter statement as they yearn for Spring. But there have been too few such days for his liking and he suddenly feels weighed down by the greyness of it all.

Although he pays little attention to the news, he cannot but be aware of the situation. He feels blessed that he cannot work from home and that nature refuses to put itself on hold while humankind tries to sort itself out. On those occasions when he has bumped into people - colleagues and visitors alike - they seem universally preoccupied with 'The Virus', their sole topic of conversation endowed with capital letters. They seem genuinely envious of his situation. He believes it is not the solitude they covet but the fact that he can find isolation so rewarding. They see nothing natural in their situation and, unlike their own versions of lockdown, recognise no hardship in his. And they may be correct, of course, but what they cannot understand is the path taken prior to him landing there; the price he has already paid. It is not as voluntary a posting as they assume. But he does nothing to disabuse them, preferring instead to acquiesce, nod knowingly, perhaps unlock a portable loo, hold a gate or two open to let them through, or indulge in the ritual of a conversation over coffee sipped from shared thermos flasks. Where's the harm in that?

*

Three years since she left and alone once again, Jonathan still struggles to establish where cooking should sit in the pecking order of his life; whether it needs to be elevated beyond a necessity. It is an idea - taking his culinary endeavours more seriously - which has always appealed to some part of him, and one which Greta certainly encouraged (though for selfish reasons). However, given the not insignificant duration since he once again began to cook meals for one, it is a question which is getting harder and harder to answer positively, layers of uninspiring routine applying matt varnish to the task and becoming increasingly difficult to shift. He is pleased that in the main he has avoided the trap of the 'ready meal' and the coincident over-reliance on the chiller section of the supermarket. At least twice a week he endeavours to cook dishes of double proportions - or normal proportions when there had been two of them - so that he can retain half for the following day or, by using old takeaway cartons, create a modest stock of back-up options in the garage chest freezer, just in case. He is not entirely sure the circumstances to which 'just in case' might apply, though recent periods of lockdown would have provided an ideal opportunity to draw on such a stock had he been compelled to totally absent himself from the world for a week or two. Were he to be paid an unexpected visit by Josh or Bernie - or even his mother come to that - there is comfort in knowing he would have no issue in feeding them, given a little judicious dipping into his reserves. Of course, what he wants more than anything else - even if he remains largely ignorant of such a desire - is to be cooking for more than just himself again, and for there to be someone else cooking for him too. Given the kitchen has been an unrewarding battleground in the past - never mind the more fundamental impact such a new arrangement would have on his life as a whole - this is a notion sprinkled with more than a little rose-tinted thinking.

As he stirs some korma sauce into a pan of part-cooked belly pork he remembers how long it had taken him to persuade Pamela as to the merits of a good curry. Not an uncommon experience, his was a pleasure discovered at University where, during his three years there, he and his friends had gradually increased the level of fire and spice to which they were prepared to subject themselves - largely in a show of bravado. Curry and beer had been natural bedfellows. In order to appeal to Pamela however he had needed to tone down his creations. Korma was as far as she would go, and although in the short-term what he came up with (she never cooked curries herself) seemed more like mild soup than anything else, its subtle flavour - with some minor tweaks - was something he came to enjoy. Looking down at the gently simmering pale yellow concoction before him, he doubts he could go back to the vindaloos of his heyday. But then there are many things to which he cannot go back, Pamela being one of them.

He sets the cooker timer to ten minutes and places a lid on the pan. Regular stirring is, he believes, one of the prerequisites of a good curry. Somewhat ironically, he fears it is one of few culinary secrets to which he has been granted access, and can't help but draw a line to a nagging sense of unfinished business with regard to Pamela, as if there were whole chunks of her life to which he was never exposed and for which he believes she still owes him an explanation. As he switches on the kettle and prepares a cafetière - one of the few refinements to which she introduced him - he wonders whether, had he been able to appreciate that essence of her which remained untapped, things might have been different. Not that there had been anything untoward in their early years together. Having fallen in love, courtship and marriage progressed as he assumed they were supposed to. Life proved itself a modest adventure; he had been happy. Surely they both had been. But at some point Pamela's shutters had begun to go up, imperceptibly at first. Jonathan now regards the second half of their marriage as death by a thousand cuts. Had the first of these been Pamela's refusal to try for children? For him, that had been as natural a next step as adding milk to the coffee he has just poured. Even though it had never been discussed - not until it was too late, one might say - it had never crossed his mind that Pamela might have other ideas. She had begged patience, found excuses; and then his own life conspired against him, primarily in the form of his father's illness. With Josh away fighting a different kind of war, he became the family's organiser-in-chief, taking on the lion's share of helping their mother come to terms with the way she would henceforth have to live her own life. Bernie had helped out from time to time, but back then she had begun to seem as if she wasn't fully committed to the real world, and when she was around her presence only served to distract Pamela further.

As he sips his coffee, he tries to recall whether he had been surprised when she announced she was leaving him. He still remembers it as no more an emotional event than a bulletin being read out on the news; more a statement of fact than anything else. She didn't want anything from him, just to be allowed to go. There was no request for money nor for a share of the house. He had asked practical questions, his head in charge over his heart; she had provided short answers where she could, evasive ones where she could not. Or where she chose not to do so. He couldn't tell the difference. It had been a strange parting from his perspective, one devoid of both necessity and emotion; yet perhaps it was also manifestation of the secrets she had kept close. Leaning towards the conventional, Jonathan suspected there was another man, or that she had a stash of money hidden away and about which he knew nothing, a parachute always ready to be called upon. He looked for the mechanisms which engineered the break-up and missed the ripping of his heart - until she had said, in an offhand manner, "it's a good job we didn't have children". Even now he wonders whether, from the very moment he had made the original suggestion of parenthood, she had been plotting her way out.

There had never been any possibility of such confusion with Greta; lack of clarity was something she failed to countenance under any circumstance. From that perspective, Jonathan always knew where he stood with her, the boundaries and potentialities of their relationship, his role within it. Had he been on the rebound when they met? How could he possibly know? From the first day she started at work - the year after Pamela's departure - Greta had swept into his life like a tornado he was entirely unable to resist. It was not merely the 'romantic' that defeated him. It was the trace of a northern European accent; the way her facial features conformed perfectly to the 'golden ratio'; her penchant for marching bra-less into his meetings, her magnificent breasts and nipples all too evident beneath the tight white shirts she tended to favour. For all that, he was essentially undone by her decisiveness. Although not the only man bowled over by her, he was the one she had chosen. Looking up from his coffee and toward the open window, he still refuses to acknowledge why. Perhaps it had been because he was three years her junior; perhaps because he represented no threat, was a 'safe bet'; perhaps she could see he was 'damaged goods', a status which absolved her of any responsibility for further destruction should things not work out - which of course they didn't when a better opportunity materialised for her. Jonathan knows he could frame their relationship in a different way, choose to see it in a more critical light, but he has established the folklore of their time together in such a way as to make it immutable: a whirlwind first few months, the sudden marriage, a road-trip honeymoon in the US, then Greta establishing herself - temporarily, as it turned out - in the very same spaces once occupied by Pamela.

Bernie had been openly critical.

"Do you know what you're doing?" she had asked the week before their wedding. "She's very - particular."

Unable not to notice the somewhat unusual choice of adjective, Jonathan assumed that Bernie would come round in the end and accept the consolation prize of being able to add Greta to her virtual cast of characters to be drawn upon one day.

"There's still time," she said.

"Time?"

"To change your mind. To call it off."

"Why should I call it off?"

As much as he loved Bernie, even today he still can't escape the sensation that, to some extent, people are lab rats to her - even if she had been unquestionably right back in 2015. And the others' view of Greta? Josh was not long out of the Army so was too preoccupied with mapping out his own future to overly care about his younger brother's; and even though she seemed just about over the death of her own husband two years earlier, his mother's opinion was inevitably disqualified on the grounds that she had adored Pamela and remained unable to reconcile herself to her abandoning them - for which she unquestionably, and quite openly, blamed Jonathan.

"2013 was such a shit year," she said once, allowing herself a rare excursion into the vernacular.

Not that anyone would disagree with her, perhaps Jonathan least of all. Was it surprising, therefore, that a year or so later he couldn't help but see Greta as an opportunity for a fresh start, in spite of what his mother and sister might think - and in spite of the ground rules Greta had very firmly laid out. Batting them aside at the time, now he cannot but regard them as conditions which bordered on the contractual: no children; one two-week foreign holiday a year with him, which he would fund; two one week holidays without him, and about which he would ask no questions. Although his role was to be that of the traditional bread-winner, responsible for assuring their general domestic comfort, her career was the more important. She argued that being older - and being a woman - meant that not only was progression harder for her, but that time was pressing too; she argued somewhat dismissively that unlike him she still had goals she wanted to achieve, and that his role was crucial in helping her get to where she needed to be. Of course she wrapped all that up in seductive language and a softer tone, and he simply went along with it. Had there been a choice? Had he heard alarm bells ringing and simply ignored them? To her credit - even after Greta had callously left him for a man who was more certain to be able to facilitate another step up the corporate ladder - Bernie never openly said "I told you so" even if it was clear that was how she felt. When he read *Poppies* for the second time, Jonathan had searched it for traces of both Pamela and Greta but found neither. "Those ghosts will appear later", he told himself. It is something he stills believes; an unveiling he dreads.

⁎

"I'm worried about him."

"Josh?"

She nods her head into the phone. "I haven't heard from him."

"No-one hears from Josh, Bernie," Jonathan says.

"I do. We've been talking. Often." She chooses not to mention she has also been speaking to Pamela - and that, as soon as the first lockdown ended they created a 'bubble' for themselves. It is proving a stimulating experience. Vindicated remarkably quickly, Bernie has already decided that Pat has a future; perhaps a role as a personal consultant or clairvoyant, or even a character in a book (an opportunity about which Pat is somewhat dubious).

"What have you been talking to him about?"

"The war. His war." She says it as flatly as she can, as if there is nothing remarkable in the statement.

Her brother is unable to mask his surprise. "He doesn't tell anyone what he went through."

"Well he's talking to me. Or has been. I" - she looks for the word - "persuaded him. It's research. Or therapy. Maybe both. Once or twice a week for a little while now, since before Christmas. Which is why I'm concerned - I haven't heard from him for about 10 days."

"You're going to write about his war?" Jonathan remains stubbornly incredulous.

"I didn't say that, Dobs. In fact, I'm not writing about Josh at all. I'm thinking of creating a character who's had similar experiences, that's all; or about someone close to them who has. Research, like I say."

Bernie thinks about waiting for the comeback, but disappointed that Jonathan is focussing on the reasons behind her conversations rather than their brother's welfare, pushes on.

"He might have had an accident," she suggests, endeavouring to bring Jonathan back to her primary concern.

He laughs. "Josh doesn't do 'accidents'. Never has from what I can recall. And if he had - well, he probably wouldn't be here now."

She has always maintained that profile of him in her mind too, but now knows - vividly, from what he has told her about Afghanistan - that it only takes one slip, one error of judgement. Everything changes in a fraction of a second.

"He works with such brutal machinery sometimes, doesn't he? I mean, chainsaws and things. What if there *had* been an accident, out in the forest somewhere, miles from anywhere. How would we know? How would anyone know?"

"Because I'm sure he has to check-in somehow. Or maybe his boss or his colleagues regularly go to see him." Jonathan tries to be consoling. "He may be our family's incarnation of Captain America, but he can't do everything on his own."

It is a joke, but she chooses not to laugh.

"Will you call him?"

"Me? What difference would that make? I mean, if he's not answering your calls..."

"I don't know. Maybe I've upset him somehow, asked too many questions. Maybe he thinks he's told me too much - or told me something he wishes he hadn't. Perhaps he doesn't trust me any more."

"And have you?"

"Have I what?"

"Gone too far, Bernie." Jonathan recalls a few incidents with Greta just before she walked out on him. "You know how direct you can be sometimes..."

She knows what he means, yet feels inclined to defend herself.

"I prefer 'honest', Dobs. Being straight with people, that's all. There's only one truth, when all's said and done." She pauses just a moment. "So will you call him?"

"As soon as you hang up."

"Thanks. And you'll text me to let me know what happens, what he says?"

"Of course."

As she waits, staring at her phone, she wonders if she actually believes what she had said to Jonathan about there only being one truth. At one level she feels the statement is logically true, but people are essentially illogical; they have feelings, opinions and perspectives. Take Pamela. Isn't she proof of the existence of a different truth, one completely at odds with that which family folklore had come to believe? Certainly different from her ex-husband's version of reality. Bernie now knows things about Jonathan that had been hidden from her, and she has an alternative take on why his relationship with Pamela failed. Only one truth? In part because of the ripples truth creates, she doesn't think so.

Her phone pings and she looks down at the newly arrived text message: 'no answer'.

*

The cabin is well insulated. Without any heating other than a wood burning stove in the lounge-cum-kitchen and a small portable radiator in the bedroom, it has to be. Winter nights can be brutal. On odd occasions when snow is piled high against the walls you can almost hear the temperature fall.

It is more than a cabin, of course. There are later incarnations of such structures - updated, expanded, located in more clement spots and glued together with the pride of a mini housing estate - which have been sold to people to use as holiday homes. A few hardier souls are permanent residents. The brochures in which they are showcased refer to them as 'luxury lodges', with exotic names and artistic photographs designed to conjure up both romantic and adventurous living experiences. Their practical aspects - triple insulation, central heating, the choice of a sauna or an external hot tub - were also emphasised, endorsed by high-quality images of internal minutiae. Shots of the surrounding forest were softened by showing the trees silhouetted against a sunrise or a sunset, and there was always at least one photograph of a semi-hidden deer or a 'resident' sitting by the large lake fishing. The snow and the biting winters were never mentioned, neither was the almost constant background music of the wind in the trees - sometimes soothing, more often than not worrying - nor the purr from a motorway close enough to the little estate to be audible on rare days when the wind chose to be still. Not that Josh's cabin is anywhere near the residential park.

Even though fishing wasn't something in which he was particularly interested, he had posed for more than one of those lake-side photographs; sitting there playing the part for an hour or so was no hardship, especially as it allowed him time to look out over the water and think - not that he remembers his thoughts from those experiences just at the moment. Communicating with a telephone mast situated on a not too-distant edge of the forest, his mobile has been ringing. Unable to precisely locate the sound, he assumes the device is somewhere in the kitchen, left lying around on the work surface. Or it could be buried in one of the pockets of his heavy coat. He hasn't the inclination to try and remember when he saw it last - nor the strength to go and find it. His wits - having not yet entirely deserted him - tell him the battery must be nearly spent. Soon it will be unable to do anything.

Had he made a mistake? That is the one question which haunts him as he drifts in and out of consciousness, memory replayed with subtitles beneath, a dream where he sees himself struggling into the snow - was it two days ago? - convinced he had succumbed to no more than a head cold, one of the perennial perils of his isolated existence. Such minor ailments had been brushed aside before. Fresh air, a couple of hours' work - even in a foot or more of snow - would surely do the trick, prove that he was above such things, that Joshua Wells didn't suffer. And he has seen real suffering. He knows what that looks like. But this? This was nothing.

Or that had been his assumption. What was unusual about a little cough when you were feeling below par? Or a shortness of breath? He had told himself to suck it up, to pull himself together; after all, he has seen men with their arms and legs blown off. And he has told Bernie about some of them.

For a while he worried that telling Bernie about Afghanistan was a kind of betrayal - of both himself and the colleagues he had lost or seen maimed. He was nervous about what she would do with what he told her, what she would write; he thought of stopping but all too soon found the experience soothing, as if it were medication of some kind, regular doses twice a week. Keep taking the tablets.

The phone. It was probably Bernie. How often had it rung? He'd lost count.

He had intended to lay down for a short while, just long enough to get the cold out of his system, but had awoken some thirteen hours later, disorientated, wheezing, his head feeling as if it was about to explode. There was a pressure in his ears that reminded him of an explosion in Kandahar, the one that tore Scottie to pieces. He hadn't yet told Bernie about Scottie. He felt as if something had been drained from him while he slept; tried to move but could not, so resolved to rest a little longer. Then the phone had rung for the first time - or was it the second, the third? He remembers being laid low by German measles when he was a child. It had been a similar experience he thinks; a vague kind of paralysis, the desire for it to be tomorrow already and the sickness over. He finds himself wishing such things once more, and before he slips back to sleep tries to imagine himself in his coat and boots, out through the door and into the snow, clearing paths, chopping wood, lighting the log burner again to warm up the cabin.

And answering the phone.

*

When Jonathan's phone rings a few days later, his immediate assumption is that it will be Bernie once again, calling to provide him with some sort of update. In the time between the third peal and when he lifts the phone from its cradle he has already constructed a scenario where Josh and Bernie have re-connected once again and Bernie has persuaded their brother to call him. "Jonathan's worried," she might have said, a white lie partly to dilute her own fears and partly to distribute familial concern more evenly. But second thoughts, arriving in the instant during which he opens his mouth and says his name, forces Jonathan to remind himself that he has never known Bernie to lie. He is still vaguely unsettled when his mother's voice surprisingly intrudes into his consciousness. "She was in pieces," he tells Bernie later that day.

Josh had been found by one of his colleagues during a routine visit. Unable to rouse him by knocking on his front door, they had tried calling him. Hearing the mobile responding inside, they then walked round the outside of the cabin, peering through windows and into the various shades of gloom beyond. Catching a glimpse of Josh static on the bed, they had resorted to brute force and charged at the back door, ripping the lock from the frame and sending splinters into the kitchen.

"They were too late, of course. It took the medics a little while to get there, but they soon confirmed he'd been gone about ten to twelve hours. There was some confusion I think, and it took a while for Josh's colleague to speak to whoever he needed to. Then they called mum. She rang me pretty much straight away."

"Poor mum."

"I know. She was on her own, of course, and as there was no way either of us could get down to her quickly I made her give me Audrey's phone number - you know, her friend from two doors down - and I got her to go and be with her. After that I had to get the doctor to her, then get in touch with Josh's work, the police, all sorts. I'm sorry I didn't call you straight away but I needed to know mum was being looked after and that whatever needed to be gone through was at least started." Jonathan pauses, conscious he has rattled through his overview. He had chosen to do so in order to forestall any questions Bernie might have had. There is a short silence. "Bernie?"

"And how are you?"

"Me?" He is thrown. Her question seems entirely inappropriate. Surely he is the least important of them all. "Okay, I suppose. I spoke to Audrey again just before I called you. The doctor's given mum something to calm her down, sedate her. I don't know. Audrey says she's bearing-up. Apparently mum said she was in some way prepared; something about having lived with the threat of such news every single day Josh was in Afghanistan."

"And we probably didn't think like that at all," Bernie observes.

Jonathan is shocked.

"Didn't you worry about him?"

"Of course! I'm not saying that. All I'm saying is that it must have been different for mum, Josh being her son and everything. There's no way we could have felt or understood that." She waits for acknowledgement but gets none. "What was it?"

"What was what?"

"What killed him, Dobs. There are" - here she hesitates - "several possibilities…"

She leaves a gap, inviting Jonathan to fill it in, to come up with his own list of possibilities. He responds quickly.

"The virus they think. No sign of anything else. They'll check of course, but they suspect he hadn't been well for a while; stuck all the way out there on his own, well, how could anyone know?"

"Which explains why he didn't answer his phone."

"Because he was too ill." Jonathan completes the thought.

"Do they know how he got it? I mean, he was hardly ever in close contact with people."

"They haven't said - and I'm not sure how they can know. Maybe it was when he went into town shopping, or he caught it from someone who came to visit the forest."

"Just bad luck then. An accident."

Jonathan remembers what he had said about Josh not 'doing' accidents. It had been a joke that was no longer funny - and no longer true.

✻

"How do you think he'll handle it?"

It is a day later. Bernie sits across from Pamela in the small sofa she has come to make her own, feet tucked beneath her, book in her lap. She has studied Pamela for a few moments before speaking, rousing the latter from her own novel.

"Jonathan?"

Bernie nods.

"Why ask me? He's your brother."

"Obviously; but I didn't live with him for seven years - not as an adult, anyway. I could guess, but even if I tried not to, part of my assessment would inevitably be informed by the little boy I *did* live with, the one who used to try and build dams in rivers with sticks and stones."

Pamela lays her book on the arm of her chair.

"I doubt I'll surprise you," she says, then pauses as if to organise her thoughts. "He'll be very organised and logical about things, of course; take on responsibility for the practical."

"Who else would?" Bernie interrupts.

"Indeed. But that would be his way in any event. He'll see it as his job. So he'll sort things out, partly - he'll say - to take the burden of your mother, but mainly because he won't be able to help himself. It's a kind of defence mechanism, I suppose; bury yourself in the nuts and bolts of things so that you don't have to worry about your emotions."

"Was he always like that?"

Pamela smiles.

"No, of course not. And I bet your little boy in shorts wasn't either!"

"Dobs?" Bernie laughs, a jumble of memories cascade at light speed through her mind. "He used to be many of the things he isn't now:

frantic, enthusiastic, ambitious, optimistic. I remember him being quick to things too. Perhaps it was because he was always trying to compete with Josh, whether he realised it or not. He wanted to be first, faster, stronger; he needed his pictures to be the best, his Lego models the tallest…though they rarely were. That kind of thing."

"Hardly the Jonathan of today."

"Hardly."

They look away from each other, Bernie down to the book lying open across her knee, Pamela up towards the window as if she has caught sight of something outside.

"Why is that, do you think?"

It is a question either one of them could have asked - though inevitably it is Bernie who does.

"I don't know. I guess he lost something along the way. Gradually. All those emotional things." Pamela frowns. "I need to be careful."

"Careful?"

"Because you might think I had a role to play. And perhaps I did. How can I not have, I suppose."

"He used to hate coming second." Bernie is astute enough to let Pamela's comment fall between them. From what both Pamela and Jonathan himself have told her, she knows enough about those seven years to have constructed a timeline for the changes in her brother during his relationship with the woman who now sits across from her. There has always been sufficient evidence to map out the cracks and fissures, the inflexion points along the way. And now, with her presence in Pamela's house - and most often in her bed - that evidence has become both more concrete and more personal. "Josh used to beat him at just about everything. He was quicker, tougher. Almost certainly brighter too. By the time they were out of shorts I suspect Dobs was already just a little tired of - something."

"That's hardly a ringing endorsement of me!" Pamela's objection is immediate and accompanied by a change of tone. "You make it sound as if I was someone - I don't know - he 'settled for'. Or that I chose him because he was - what? - a loser."

Bernie shakes her head gently.

"You, my dear, were his saviour. I don't think he was ever happier than when he was with you. You gave him the chance to be the man he had the potential to be - just as you have given me something similar." She waits to see if there is any response. The younger woman glances down at her book and Bernie feels the tension dissipate. Bordering on forty, she wonders if her extra five years have given her a kind of wisdom. Or is it something else, an amalgamation of unlocked experience and the inevitable bequest of everything that led to *Poppies*, plus an appreciation of the future? "The fact that he eventually resigned himself to being the person he is today is not down to you. How could it be?"

There is a silence brought about by Bernie's rhetorical question which suddenly wraps itself about them, enveloping the room and all it contains. It is as if cotton wool has materialised to cocoon and protect them. They look around, avoiding each other's glance even though they know the moment of danger has passed.

"Isn't it odd?" says Pamela.

"What?"

"That Josh has just died and here we are talking about Jonathan."

"Odd? I don't think so, not really. In my experience you can't talk about any one of us without including the others. In the same way, in whatever I write, Jonathan and Josh - and now you - will always be there, somewhere, like invisible hands guiding me."

"Or ghosts," suggests Pamela.

"Or ghosts."

*

So what were they now, those who were left?

Spring arrived hesitantly, as if Josh's passing had given it permission to emerge from its own isolation, tentatively projecting fingers of light onto the earth with promises of warmth, an optimism suggesting things would start to get better. Jonathan wondered how you might measure those; know; be certain.

He had been surprised how stoical their mother had been. By the day of the funeral it was as if she had already indulged her grief, worked it through before she needed to see them, as if overt sadness was an embarrassing blemish which required surgical removal. Unaware of her resolve, he had tiptoed around her at first, wary of indulging in too much reminiscence, busying himself with practicalities and organisation. He kept telling himself that it was important things went smoothly. Three of Josh's old comrades had presented themselves at the church; in full uniform they leant proceedings a gravitas and solemnity that seemed to fit with the post-Army Josh he had come to know, the one who had lived on after his war. They endowed events with a seriousness which conferred importance and respect upon the man who was not there. The only time his mother had shown any signs of breaking down was when she had first seen them, resplendent as if newly minted, slowly walking up the path towards the narthex. Perhaps in slow step like that they had reminded her of how she had lived through those years fully expecting to one day find herself following Josh's coffin shrouded in the Union flag and borne aloft by six from his regiment perfectly attired and perfectly in unison. If so, seeing them out of step, almost at their ease, might have offered her some comfort, the reward of knowing that earlier catastrophe - and the formal pageant it would have inevitably spawned - had been avoided. It might just have been enough to see her through the day.

"He was lucky really," she says to Jonathan out of nowhere as they walk slowly away from the crematorium, the formal car waiting to take them back to her house where Audrey was busy putting the finishing touches to the small tea on which they had settled.

He lets it go, partly because he is unsure how to respond, and partly because his eye is draw once again to Bernie and Pamela walking slightly ahead of them; Pamela's arm is round Bernie's waist, his sister's head slightly inclined toward his ex-wife's shoulder. He had been taken aback when the two of them had emerged from the same car, accepting a kiss on the cheek from Pamela as if they were old friends brought together by sad circumstance. His mother had embraced her as if there had been no passage of time since they had last seen each other, and as the four of them congregated outside the church waiting for the hearse, he was struck how an outsider could easily have taken them for siblings - he, Bernie and Pamela - his mother behaving as if they all belonged to her. He wanted to ask his mother when she had last seen Pamela, but chooses not to do so; it seems inappropriate.

"You don't mind, Dobs?" Bernie had asked him once she had released him from her initial hug.

"Mind?"

"That Pammy's here. I needed some moral support."

It was a statement that seemed to short-circuit all the questions and answers that should have preceded it, and as such left Jonathan attempting to draw conclusions, build his own narrative. All of which was Bernie's territory of course, and he found himself adrift as a result. Striving for some kind of resolution had forced his detachment from proceedings a little, and seeing them walking just ahead of him simply confirms he is yet to successfully conclude his study.

"Will you miss him?"

Jonathan is standing in the back garden examining the naked borders, knowing that beneath their dull brown surface his mother's perennials are stirring. In a month it will be greener; in three or four, a riot of colour. He feels Bernie's hand slip through his arm before he hears her voice.

"Of course," he replies. "Even though we didn't see that much of each other, it was comforting to know he was there if we ever needed him."

"I suppose so," she says, evidently unconvinced, "though I do wonder if he would ever have changed."

"Changed? How?"

"Oh, got over his war. Reconciled himself to it and what he experienced; put it behind him. Phrase it however you like."

"You don't think he had?" Jonathan makes to walk down the garden but she holds him in place.

"Do you?"

"Northumberland; his forests. I got the impression he'd found what he was looking for. He seemed - I don't know - happy enough."

Bernie laughs gently, as if she is humouring him.

"When do you last remember Josh really happy?" It is a question she could have asked of any of them. In her mother's case happiness would surely have accompanied Josh's leaving the Army, but after that? She wonders about herself too, feeling as if she is close to something, yet fundamentally unsure how relevant being happy is. She returns to her theme. "I mean, really happy, Dobs? Because I can't." Her brother inclines his head; a sign he is either agreeing with her or inviting her to go on. "That's not to say he couldn't have been. But I don't buy that notion that he had found himself. He was still running away from his past, joining the dots as to what it had done to him."

"He told you that?"

"In a way. It was in his voice when he talked about Afghanistan; in the stories, the atrocities, the pain. I heard it most when he talked about other soldiers, people he knew who hadn't been as lucky as he had, those who hadn't got out in time. There was a part of him that couldn't understand why they had been singled out to suffer and he hadn't; that was the version of Josh who struggled with luck and fate and chance, what happened one day to the next. In the desert, I mean. That's one of the reasons the forest suited him so well: there was no similar chance or fate for him to worry about. Seasons happened, trees grew. It was predictable. There were never any alternatives to concern him." She pauses long enough to acquiesce to their moving down the garden. "I think he was beginning to see a glimmer of light at the end of the tunnel, simply because he had taken the brave step of sharing."

"Your conversations."

She nods her head, releasing his arm as she does so. What does she see when she looks into the borders? More stories unfolding.

"Was it too little too late? I hope not."

They walk on in silence until they reach the trellis that partially shields them from their mother's modest vegetable patch.

"And what about us, Bernie?" Jonathan asks. It is a question that surprises her.

"Us?"

"Is it too late for us, Bernie? Haven't we been fighting our own wars, our private battles? Don't we each have wounds to tend? Doesn't there come a point when we say that we've had enough of trying?"

She smiles at him.

"That's unusually philosophical for you, Dobs."

"Well if you can't be philosophical at a funeral, when can you be?"

It is not meant as a joke but Bernie laughs nonetheless. She reattaches herself to his arm, turns him around, and begins to steer him back toward the house.

"And where are your scars, brother mine?"

"They're obvious aren't they? Take your pick. You arrived here with one of them."

"Ah."

She suddenly finds herself not in the mood to explain or analyse; the former would take too long, and the later be a fruitless exercise. Would Jonathan be able to take it all in, process and understand it? There is nothing she can say that might fill the gap she now senses between the two of them. Having lost one person who acted as a bridge between them, Bernie realises Josh has been replaced by another; but Pamela comes with a different history, in some ways a less innocent one. What had Jonathan said all those months ago about playing in the river when they were children? That was the kind of history which easily morphs into legend. Perhaps Pamela may find herself in the same category at some point in the future, finding an occasion to bring them together, one which permits sharing, honesty, the philosophical. But now is not the time. It is too early; so much of their history has yet to be written. And, if she is honest with herself, she finds it difficult to commit to the off-the-cuff; though she feels she is trying, it is not an environment where she feels able to work things through. She needs quiet, blank sheets of paper, and to be supported by characters she has yet to invent.

"When are you off?" Jonathan chooses not to pursue her evasion.

"We've a train booked a little after four."

He can't help but remark the confidence in the way she said 'we'.

"Do you want a lift to the station?"

"There's a taxi already booked. And anyway, that's probably for the best, don't you think?" It is a cryptic comment from which she swerves back to the mundane. "One more cup of tea before we go?"

Jonathan watches Bernie as she leaves his side and walks back into the house. It is, he realises, a house he has never liked. After Devon and his grandmother's - when they were all still together - his mother's current house, smaller, unremarkable, stands as a monument to loss. She is here because their grandfather died, then their grandmother, then their father. And then, one by one, the three of them choose to leave her - and now Josh has gone altogether. It is a house into which his mother has been forced, beating a retreat through no fault of her own.

When was Josh happy? That had been Bernie's question. When were any of them last that way, his mother included? He looks back down the brown garden and to the brown trellis, and he remembers a magical garden with a river beyond it and children building dams in the sunshine.

Park'n'Ride

She speaks with a strange intonation, a peculiar rise and fall in her voice as if the person who taught her English had overlaid upon it the rhythms and inflections of an entirely different language: French, or German, or Pig Latin. It also seems she has never acquainted herself with the full suite of letters in the alphabet; some are intermittently missing, certain combinations compromised. And occasionally, unsure she has got her meaning across, she replays whole phrases - most often with no alteration in the words used or their sequence, as if repetition is the guarantor of understanding.

"I 'ad chips for dinner, I did. Chips for dinner. Those wavy ones. The ones like waves. But if you cooks 'em for too long they gets crispy on the outside, and I don't like crispy chips. Not when I 'ave 'em for me dinner."

Her voice accosts him from over his shoulder. Sitting at the front of the tram, he places her perhaps four rows behind him, the tone of her voice slicing through the air between them as if that were no distance at all, as if she is almost in his ear. He wants to turn and look, to assign a physical form to the voice. Perhaps doing so will remove the threat.

"Me boyfriend, 'e likes chips an' all. But not those wavy ones. So I 'as to do two lots when he comes round for dinner, 'cos he don't like those wavy ones. Says they're a waste of space, whatever that means. They're just chips, ain't they? Chips for dinner."

It is a voice that defies age. He imagines it belongs to someone who is younger than himself; there is a slovenliness about it he can only attribute to youth. Yet there is also something else; not wisdom - how could it be?! - but an undercurrent which suggests experience above maturity, experience in the sense of having lived for many years, nothing more. He roots this new notion in the way she says 'boyfriend'. It is not spoken from the flush of youth, but with a brash awareness suggestive of someone who is cognisant they are crossing a boundary, stealing a word from another vocabulary, one to which they should not be party. Experience not maturity.

"Sausages 'e likes. Beef ones. It's 'ard to get beef sausages these days, ain't it? 'E don't like all those fancy sausages wiv fancy flavours, me boyfriend don't. Not wiv apple or onion or whatnot. 'E likes beef. And it's 'ard to get your 'ands on beef sausages, ain't it? Used to be easy. Used to be all there was when I was a girl, beef sausages. Got 'em from the butchers at the end of our road; the one wot ain't there no more. Lovely sausages 'e 'ad, that butchers. Me boyfriend would 'ave loved those, 'e would."

It is an assertion which places her in time. She is older than she sounds, older than the language she uses - and he wants to turn round even more as a result. He finds himself guessing. She is probably older than forty based on what she has just said, and he instinctively feels the need to bestow more years on her - yet finds himself unable to do so without evidence.

"Yes."

It is another voice; a companion piece. He wonders if the out-of-balance exchange is one in which this second person has been innocently trapped; as if they simply took a spare seat on a tram and found themselves adopted. It is a 'yes' delivered by someone without choice. Hidden in that single word is an implicit desire for the tram to go faster - or for the voluble woman to get off at the next stop. It is a 'yes' that contains more of the 'no' in it; a 'yes' that is a plea for help, an unspoken desire to be rescued.

"I don't mind 'em, sausages. But I likes fish fingers bet'er. 'Specially wiv wavy chips. But me boyfriend, 'e don't like fish fingers; so when 'e comes round for dinner I 'as to cook two lots of chips *and* sausages *and* fish fingers, 'cos if I didn't what would we eat, eh?"

Attempting to block her out, he tries to focus on the city centre as it subsides into suburbs: a terrace or two, the hint of a new development, tired offices, a park and a school beyond. The tram stops three more times, and even though he tries not to listen he is unable not to collect the words she insists on repeating. 'Boyfriend' accosts him like a slap round the face, as does 'shopping' when she makes a partial segue away from the subject of her dinner.

"I likes Asda, I do. Sometimes I goes to Morrison's 'cos there's one just round the corner, but I likes Asda better. And B&M. That B&M's good for some things. But not sausages. Asda's good for sausages. My boyfriend likes 'is sausages from Asda."

And even though the topics have varied a little, the way she relays them creates a blur, a noise lacking any distinction.

The 'ding' of the bell causes him to look up to where the 'Stopping' sign has been illuminated once more, and as the tram slows he realises he can no longer hear her. He is aware of the second voice saying 'Bye', and cannot help but register the relief embodied in the word.

When the tram stops it is outside a small parade of shops. Ahead, he can see a supermarket - Morrison's - squeezed between two charity shops, a Clinton's cards, a bookmakers. Another shop front is whitewashed and boasts a 'To Let' sign that hangs slightly askew. He waits.

A woman appears by his window and pauses before crossing towards the shops. He knows it is her. He catches her in profile for a moment and is surprised. She is at least fifty - if not much older - with a face worn down by living, the naïve juggling of the everyday. Cocooned in a too-familiar grey raincoat, she tugs a dilapidated shopping trolley behind her, its left wheel slightly out of alignment.

Her walk is a shuffle; she stoops a little; her hair, grey and wispy, looks too thin to be controllable.

As she reaches the far pavement, the doors of the tram slide to a close, and he feels the soft jolt of motion. Protected now, he can turn his head to watch her, and just before she disappears from view he sees her accost a pedestrian who just happens to be heading her way. And he imagines a story about chips and sausages being re-told as if buried within it are the secrets of the universe.

Damage

No-one had ever told her she was beautiful. Not said it and meant it. There had been lots of boys who'd said something similar, assuming flattery and a kind word was all it took to be rewarded with her favours. And sometimes it had, but usually only when she was lonely or bored or victim of a little too much wine on a Saturday evening. If she worked late, as she sometimes did, her encounters with friends were shaped by the fact that they had already been drinking for a while, served in bars by someone just like her. When she was in the mood she would strive to join in with the bonhomie and general abandon, that was when their flattery worked best. But sooner or later she would realise they were just boys with no real interest in her; no interest in anything but satisfying themselves. Sometimes this realisation would occasionally dawn on mornings when she would wake up somewhere new; strangely homogenous bedrooms even though each and every one of them was unique. More than once she had woken in the middle of the night in such places and found herself swamped by the drab certainty of having made another mistake and so slipped away before dawn. Once or twice enlightenment took a little longer; it had taken nearly four months before she saw through Sam - though catching him in bed with a mutual acquaintance was what really drew back the veil. Perhaps that had been the lowest point of all. So she had berated herself, told herself to 'get a grip' and 'pull herself together' - a mantra which worked well enough for a while until she became bored or lonely once again.

Yet if you had asked her what she was looking for, softened your words to make the enquiry seem as caring as possible, she would have struggled to articulate her goal, in all probability telling you precisely what it wasn't rather than what it was: not drifting from one shit waitressing job to the next; not getting paid peanuts for working her arse off; and not being weak when it came to giving in too easily. Not that she was that kind of girl. Unlike Abi who was in many ways her yardstick, the epitome of what she was determined to never let herself become. Careless Abi whose judgement was worse than anyone's, whose capacity for reckless abandonment seemed to know no bounds, and who would regularly chide her for failing to 'let her hair down'. Three years in the UK and, even if she had not entirely lost her East European accent, Kara's knowledge of English colloquialisms was sufficiently substantive to know what people really meant most of the time. To be any good working in restaurants and bars she'd had to learn quickly, the textbook language she'd been fed at school inadequate in such environments.

Which was one of the reasons she'd been taken aback when he'd said "you know, Kara, you are beautiful". Not only had no-one ever said that to her before, he had said it properly, meaningfully, without resorting to slang or swearing; the words he used passed the test of being 'grown-up', 'adult'. Perhaps above all else, they had been understood - not by her, but by him. And he had said them without any apparent devious intent or self-serving ambition. She truly believed he had spoken - "you know, Kara, you are beautiful" - because he was being honest. Yet even taking all this into account, what surprised her most of all was the notion itself, his premise. How could he say such a thing, applying a quality to her against which - in her own estimation - she fell so far short? She thought, for example, that her face was slightly too broad, her nose slightly too large; she had always assessed as her hair as being a little too straight; she felt her build a tad stocky and her thighs a little fat - a fact of which she was reminded every time she forced herself into the tight pairs of black jeans restaurants and bars tended to insist she wore. "It helps take the punters' minds off the crap food" a bar manager had told her once. In her more generous moments - and in spite of the myriad of 'too this' or 'too that' with which she labelled herself - she was prepared to concede she was passable enough and that her figure was decent. She knew she looked good in a bikini for example, and when she really made an effort - make-up, the works - then maybe the mirror might award her seven-out-of-ten. But 'beautiful'? That was nine-out-of-ten territory!

There were lots of girls like her of course: Caro, Anna, Trudi. To her they all seemed slimmer, prettier, and made the most out of what they had been gifted. Anna, now pregnant for the second time, hadn't wasted a day since she'd arrived in England with Kara and the others, a little squadron of university-educated Europeans landing at Gatwick and seeking Nirvana. Anna's plan was the most clearly defined, and she was prepared to use whatever tactic required to see it through. Toby, who she'd met after three months' working in Brighton, hadn't really stood a chance, seduced by her easy manner and the way her accent caressed words and made his native language seem exotic. Kara had met him briefly the last time Anna had come north for a reunion, the four of them dispersed around the country soon enough, eventually needing to resort to coordinated and therefore infrequent catch-ups to compare notes and geography. Inevitably Kara judged Sam against Toby if only to try and assess how close she had been to fulfilling her own version of 'the dream' - or to confirm that she'd had a lucky escape. Like Sam, Toby seemed little more than a boy: yes, he was older than Anna by a couple of years, and yes, he had a good job in the city which funded their semi-detached suburban lifestyle; nonetheless to Kara he was little more than a youth. In comparison - and even taking all Sam's plus points into consideration - her conclusion was that she'd had a lucky escape. When they had all last met, Sam had been old news and, in consequence, her debrief on the state of her love life amounted to no more than a perfunctory update. Sitting outside a canal-side pub in Nottingham (it being Caro's turn to act as 'hostess'), Kara's seismic event - "you know, Kara, you are beautiful" - was still four months hence; she had no more chance of predicting that than the winning lottery numbers, a crossed-fingers two-pounds-a-week addiction she tolerated because it kept alive the dream of having the freedom to experience life through a lens that didn't involve reliance on a Sam or a Toby.

Having tried working (adopting a portfolio of jobs similar to Kara's own), Caro had eventually returned to studying. Ever since they'd arrived in England, she had confessed to feeling unfulfilled academically in spite of the degree she'd gained before leaving home; so she found herself a post-graduate course at Nottingham University, indulging her passion for ancient history. If she rarely spoke about men it was either because they didn't much matter to her or because she was an ultra-private person. Kara was unable to be certain which it was, but knowing Caro found her studies totally absorbing, favoured the former. What she had in common with Anna was that, in their different ways, they were living out their dreams - as Trudi would soon be once she had completed her nurse's training in Bristol. Leaving Nottingham that Sunday evening (the last time they had been together) how could Kara feel anything other than that she was the odd-one-out, still adrift with no course plotted?

He had become a regular at the café - even though it wasn't a particularly special café at all, but rather a tea room attached to the municipal art gallery. On perhaps his second or third visit he had told her he didn't like chain coffee shops because, although they were friendly enough, he felt the staff were just going through the motions, and, as a patron, he was entirely inconsequential. The gallery's tea room was a more personal experience, a 'one off'. He said he loved art and, even though the main displays changed infrequently, liked to visit regularly; for him, the real joy came from the two rooms used for temporary exhibitions and which in consequence were in a general state of flux. Finding something new was always wonderful. So she got used to seeing him, initially perhaps twice a month, and then recently as much as twice a week. She became familiar with what he ordered depending on whether he was visiting in the morning or the afternoon; the day she had suggested Earl Grey and a scone (no cream!) before he had requested them prompted his first use of her name, clearly visible on her royal blue and gold badge.

He was not the only regular patron of the tea room, nor the only one who used her name. Kara liked her regulars, their friendliness; she liked knowing something about them, the titbits they shared with her helped form a connection, their reward being a little extra attention when she was able to offer it. There were the Clarke sisters who turned up on the first Wednesday of every month, travelling from the opposite sides of the city to spend the morning triangulating their lives. Often, Jane (the younger of the two) would say "it looks like a three-pot morning today, Kara" - a sign that she and her elder sibling would chat on through until lunchtime. And Mr Bostock who broke into his pension every Thursday morning with tea - "nice and strong, Kara!" - and two well-browned crumpets. If the sisters and Mr Bostock helped provide a drumbeat to her working week, then the sporadic and unpredictable appearance of her new admirer offered a lift to her day. And was that he was, an admirer? It sounded an unwholesome appellation, though one she was fairly sure Caro or Trudi would use if she told them about him. Anna would probably surface a more agricultural term! But would she tell them? After all, what was there to tell, really?

She knew little about him beyond his preferences for comestibles and tea, although he had confessed his name - Charles (he hated 'Charlie'!) - and that he was a University lecturer 'on sabbatical'. It was a phrase which had immediately prompted questions; conscious of her position, they remained unasked. If you were to have caught sight of him across a gallery floor what would you have seen? A man probably in his forties, impeccably dressed with a penchant for tweed jackets and matching waistcoats. His shirts were always plain but never dull, with a preference for the blue end of the spectrum, their shades ranging from the most subtle pastels to the garishly bold. He usually wore brown shoes - well polished brogues seemed his favourite - and between the shoes and the jacket, trousers that were nearly always casual but never slovenly. Kara had categorised his face as 'kind' from very early on. It was slightly elongated and angular, and she never saw him anything other than clean shaven. Circular-rimmed glasses adorned his nose behind which lively dark brown eyes would scan the scene. His hair, parted to one side and swept back, was longer than fashionable and, though also brown, already betrayed early traces of grey. To Kara it seemed entirely appropriate that Earl Grey should be his favourite type of tea - not that she had any idea what an Earl should look like! And that was how she occasionally thought of him, an Earl. Yes, he looked entirely like a university lecturer, and Caro probably had numerous tutors who fitted the same identikit profile; yet Kara knew there had to be more to him than that, after all he was as far removed from the likes of Toby and Sam as it was possible to be. Overall, he had the air of a man who knew things - perhaps himself most of all. He looked intelligent and gave the impression that when he walked around the gallery he would know what he was looking at. There was nothing frivolous or superficial in his demeanour, which inevitably suggested a sense of purpose. Here was a powerful combination - this capacity for seriousness and knowledge, allied to Kara's simple assessment that he seemed 'kind' - which endowed his words with weight. So how could he not have meant it when he said "you know, Kara, you are beautiful"? After all, did he not understand what beauty was? Had the many hours spent pacing the gallery (and other galleries elsewhere, Kara assumed) not qualified him to be able to say what was - and what was not - beautiful? There could be nothing superficial about him from that perspective.

Others might point to his jackets and waistcoats and accuse him of being showy; they might raise an eyebrow at the way he insisted on keeping his hair a little on the long side; they might ask the question Kara felt unable to - exactly what did 'on sabbatical' mean? - and do so with a knowing timbre in their voice.

Yet Kara did none of those things, which in itself raised a question which required answering. She liked him as a customer in the same way that she liked Mr Bostock or the Clarke sisters - indeed as she preferred to think she liked all her customers - but from the moment that afternoon when she placed his tea and scone in front of him as he sat at his favourite table in the corner of the tea room and told her she was beautiful, what then? Something happened at that point. He was no longer 'Charles, her customer'; he became someone else, if for no other reason than at some unknown point Kara had, for him, ceased to be simply the girl who served him tea.

His change of status did not arise simply because he had called her beautiful, but because of the process leading up to that moment: he had noticed her, marked her out, individualised her, examined her as he might have a painting on the gallery walls; at some point she had ceased to be anonymous and became 'Kara', with qualities he deemed needed recognition. Inevitably this meant how she saw him had to change too. In her head the voices of Anna, Caro and Trudi fought to have their say, overlaying their own experiences and prejudices, jumping to their own conclusions. Anna, the mercenary one, would tell her to make hay while the sun shone, and use terms like 'Sugar Daddy', encouraging Kara to take advantage of the situation for who knew where it might lead? Caro might shrug her shoulders and tell her that the world was full of such men, most of whom were only feigning intellectual superiority; she might say that once you scratched the surface, the veneer inevitably ended up behind your fingernails; so Kara should be wary, run a mile. Always the considerate one - as her chosen profession demanded - Trudi's view would be more balanced, more romantic. Harbouring an unspoken desire to be swept off her feet one day by dashing young doctor, there were elements in Kara's story that played to her own dreams. Unable to resolve the contrary views, Kara's predicament remained solely her own.

How many factors did she need to consider? And if she were weighing them on some kind of scale, how would she define the extremes - and what would tip the balance either way? He had said "you know, Kara, you are beautiful" as if it were an incontrovertible fact that simply needed stating; he had not followed it with anything other than a smile, turning his attention to buttering his scone. He appeared to have expected nothing from her as a consequence of his statement - presumably other than the inevitable blush on her cheeks - and had not pressed her further. As far as she could see there appeared to be no motivation other than to register a truth, and neither was it the first move in an opening gambit. It was as if an invisible full stop after 'beautiful' brought the matter to an end. Had it done so, from his perspective? How could it from hers? If the ground had shifted between them - for her at least - how did she now feel about him? Had his words loosed any stirrings of attraction? There could be no doubt that he was a reasonably handsome man, even if his was the persona of a slightly outdated 'cavalier intellectual'; perhaps ten years earlier he might have been at his peak - and five years before that entirely irresistible. But if he was in his early forties as Kara suspected, then he was almost old enough to be her father, and this endowed Anna's imagined 'Sugar Daddy' comment with a second meaning. But Kara told herself age wasn't the primary consideration here. What if he had followed up his statement with something else, a proposal, a suggestion? The offer of dinner perhaps, couched in such a way as to seem logical, generous, unthreatening. Under those circumstances she would have been pressed into something entirely binary. Deciding which way to jump would have forced the application of a fresh lens onto his declaration of her beauty - one which confirmed she accepted what he said at face value, or one which dismissed his words as a cheap and grubby salvo.

As it transpired, she had limited time for deliberation. He next crossed the tea room's threshold just two days later, and with less than half-an-hour before it was due to close. Kara was already well into her routine of cleaning the tables to ensure they would be ready for the following morning when something made her look up from where she was working. Charles paused at the door, then, having caught her eye, made his way to his usual table. Surprised to see him there - around three o-clock was his normal arrival time for afternoon visits - she wiped her hands on her apron and walked over to where he sat. Although from a distance he appeared no different to normal, once she was standing across the table from him it was evident something was amiss; he had clearly not shaved since she had seen him last, and his jacket-shirt combination lacked its usual harmony.

"I'm afraid all the scones are gone," she offered, trying to focus on her role.

"Of course," he replied with a tired smile. "Just a coffee will be fine, Kara, thank you."

"Coffee?"

"Please."

He never drank coffee in the afternoon. As she walked back to the counter, she wondered if the coffee was to keep him awake, or perhaps there had been some bad news and he had been knocked out of kilter - hence the timing of the visit, his appearance, his choice of beverage.

"He's late today isn't he?" said Angie as she passed Kara the coffee, nodding in Charles' direction. "Ten more minutes and I wouldn't have served him."

Placing the cup on a tray with a small pot of milk and bowl of sugar - even though she knew he required neither - Kara wondered if he had indeed arrived ten or more minutes later whether she would have gone behind the counter and prepared his drink herself.

She put the coffee, milk and sugar on the table in front of him along with the bill. Charles glanced at the assemblage, smiled just a little, then looked up at her.

"Thank you, Kara." Then, as she turned to go and resume her end-of-day chores, he said, "Actually, I wonder if I might have a word." It was enough for her to stop and look back at him. He registered the look on her face. "Not now, obviously. But once you've finished here. Just five minutes. I'll wait outside. If you don't mind. Please."

The gallery was set back from the road. A three-storey u-shaped construction designed to look older than it actually was, it embraced a small stone-flagged courtyard with a fountain at its centre; between the fountain and the building, six wooden benches stood guard. Often, when the weather was good, tea room patrons might ask for their drinks to be served in takeaway-style cups and their food on paper plates so that they could sit outside in the sun. The gallery management had debated the possibility of upgrading the simple benches to proper tables and chairs thereby positively encouraging people to use the courtyard as an official extension of the café. Although no decision had yet been taken, in Angie's view it was "just a matter of time", bemoaning the likelihood of having more people to serve, more distance to cover, and not being paid a penny extra for doing so.

Having completed her work slightly more rapidly than usual - and eschewing the customary end-of-day chit-chat with Angie - Kara emerged from the building some forty minutes later to find Charles sitting on a bench in the left-hand corner of the courtyard. He waved, briefly and unnecessarily.

"Are you okay?" She had come to a halt in front of him.

"Please." He motioned to the vacant space alongside him.

Kara hesitated for a moment, long enough to assess size of the gap and how far she would be from him. Once sitting down, she looked out towards the road, establishing her bearings to it, clarifying her route should she need to make a rapid getaway. On the pavement, people were making their way home from work, and the two nearby bus stops had small queues forming. Feeling secure, she turned to look at him. His head was bowed slightly; he seemed to be focussed on his hands which were resting in his lap.

"I wanted," he said without moving, "to apologise." Then he looked up. "For what I said the other day. It was - inappropriate. I'm sorry."

She was instantly confused, though not to what he was referring.

"That's okay. I mean, I didn't take offence or anything." She expected him to smile, to show some sign of relief.

"Good." He paused. "But it was still wrong of me to say what I said."

"Wrong? You mean it wasn't true?"

She wasn't sure what hit her the hardest: the idea that he had lied to her, or the possibility that she wasn't beautiful after all but rather - as she had always believed - plain and ordinary. As she juggled both notions for a split second, it became clear that neither would be without collateral damage.

"No. Of course not." Seeing the concern on her face, Charles tried a smile. "It was absolutely true. You are... But that doesn't alter the fact that I shouldn't have said it, compliment or otherwise. And certainly not in your working environment where you could have no opportunity respond as you might have wished. You would have been perfectly justified in slapping my face... It was actually a selfish thing to say. I said it more for my own benefit than yours, I fear; as if I was proving something to myself, how clever and mature I was, and without any regard as to how you might react." Prompted by his own words, he paused to allow her to respond. She did not. "It only hit me later that evening. I went from feeling smug, very pleased with myself, to being absolutely horrified at what I'd done. And all in a heartbeat. I wanted to apologise immediately, but couldn't. I wanted to come yesterday to do so, but couldn't. This is the first chance I've had, though the damage may have already been done."

"Damage?"

"To me, certainly - but I don't care about that. But to you. What must you have thought of me, or of yourself even? What might my words have made you think, or do? One can't say anything like that - or anything at all really - without there being consequences of some kind. I only hope they haven't been too great. For you, that is. And that you'll forgive me."

There was no point in denying the train of thought initiated by what he had said. All that self-analysis, the asking 'what if?', the internal dialogues with her friends; undoubtedly he had been responsible for those. But 'damage'? Kara wasn't sure about that. Had a revised consideration of herself - all predicated around the word 'beautiful' - been harmful in any way? She doubted it. Perhaps the opposite. If it allowed her to take a more positive view of herself, wasn't that - generally at least - a good thing? And had he not just reaffirmed his statement? If it was as true now as it had been two days ago did that not make it even more powerful? Whether or not he should have made the declaration in the first instance was another matter entirely, Kara understood that. Saying something so unexpected, so personal, so out-of-the-blue, was unconventional to put it mildly. And he *had* placed her in a difficult position, that she could not deny, his words perhaps backing her into a corner. But 'damage'? Perhaps to him; she could see that. Unshaven and - by his standards - vaguely dishevelled, he had clearly taken the potential consequences of his action to heart, its negative repercussions self-inflicted.

A large cream-and-blue bus pulled up at the bus stop, dragging her attention away from him. Kara watched two people get off and then the bus swallow the entirety of the queue that had formed.

"You don't need to apologise," she said, still looking away, watching as an elderly lady, just disembarked, struggled to get her shopping trolley under control before shuffling slowly away towards the centre of the town. She looked back at him; his face seemed suddenly hopeful. "It was a nice thing to say - even if it did take me by surprise. For all sorts of reasons."

A frown appeared on his forehead and Kara could see Charles fighting back the desire to delve, to ask her what she meant. It was a question she had no desire to hear, never mind answer.

"So please don't worry about it. No damage done. Not to me at any rate."

They both fell silent - Kara because she had nothing else to add, and Charles because he dared not to. It felt a little like a truce, even though such a thing was inappropriate given there had been no hostilities. Quite the opposite, in a way.

But it was time to move on. Kara felt as if she had managed to draw a line under the incident, a boundary which freed them both; her to carry on with her humdrum life, Charles to forgive himself. She stole a glance at him. He was now looking toward the road, and she had a sense of a weight having been lifted from his shoulders. She could imagine him going home, shaving, ensuring he had the right clothes ready for the day that would follow this one; perhaps he might even be reenergised, who could say. Anything was possible.

And whether he realised it or not, he had given her something precious too; Kara now saw herself in a different light, a better, more positive one. Certainly she had told him not to apologise, but what she had not done was to thank him. Didn't "you know, Kara, you are beautiful" deserve recognition of some kind? Would it not be right to ensure the scales were balanced so that any notion of 'damage' was expelled for good?

"There's a new exhibition opening on Monday," she found herself saying. "Eastern European painters and sculptors. Are you planning to come and see it?"

He smiled.

"To be honest, I wasn't entirely sure." He paused. "If you had been upset with me then I wouldn't have been able to forgive myself. Under those circumstances I wasn't sure if I'd ever be able to come back here again." He glanced around the courtyard with the air of a man who could have been saying goodbye - and was relieved not to be doing so.

"I don't work Mondays," Kara said. "Perhaps I could see the exhibition with you and then you could tell me what I was looking at and explain things about my countrymen I don't already know."

He laughed.

"I suspect you know far more than you let on, Kara."

"Well, there's only one way to find out isn't there?" And she laughed too. It was laughter that allowed her to stand and smile, and with a slight wave of her hand, to walk away.

Downsizing

There was a game they used to play: "if you had been a character from a novel, who would have written the book?" He liked to joke his creator would have been Hemingway and that he'd be hard-drinking, hard-smoking, tough and rough - and he did so knowing he was nothing like that. As did she. In her case she hadn't chosen Austen as he suspected she might, but rather Woolf, saying she saw herself as slightly wan and scatty, but intellectual and interesting with it. When he suggested she'd be more at home in *The Old Curiosity Shop* she feigned a swipe at him.

But life wasn't like a novel; at least not theirs. Not in the way they thought a novel should be.

They had met not because of a novelist but thanks to a poet. Eliot had been required reading during their first term at Southampton: "we like to throw people in at the deep end" their tutor had boasted. Where Kate had been able to swim, Patrick struggled to keep afloat, and her providing him with the occasional literary arm-bands inevitably brought them together. As if to justify her selection of the creator of her novel-persona, Kate would later tease him that their courtship had been closer to Woolf than Hemingway; his standard rebuttal, subsequently in use for many years, was that Henry James was more likely to have been the culprit on the basis that it took them so long to get anywhere. The first time he used the joke she had thumped him on the arm, and it became their own little Vaudeville routine. When did the friendly punches stop being thrown? Patrick tells himself he can't recall, even though he knows precisely the year, month, day and minute.

And now, since that first Eliot-driven encounter, over fifty-five years have passed and tomorrow is their Golden Wedding anniversary.

He has nothing particular planned. There had been a time when they celebrated every passing year as if adding to their stock of achievements, as if each individual twelve months was a remarkable triumph in itself. And then the motivation for the cakes and cards shifted to give their children a chance to go to town; the seventeenth of July became like an extra birthday, an excuse for a party. How long did that last? Patrick knows not long enough. Those more family-oriented affairs began when Sarah was six and Henry four, but then - in the blink of an eye! - they were fifteen and thirteen and starting to have other things on their minds. Rather than let the ceremony suffer a painful and slow death, the month before their eighteenth anniversary Kate suggested "let's not do the wedding anniversary thing this year, eh?" Neither of the children complained, and even though Patrick felt it was signalling the end of something, he said nothing. For him it symbolised a turning point, as if all their lives they had been scrambling up to a peak of some kind and were now heading down the other side. Then, in rapid succession, the kids seemed to race into and out of sixth form, into and out of university; the house became a refuge for them out of term time, and later little more than an occasional holiday home. When they started their own families it became less than that.

Kate started talking about 'downsizing'. She had thrown it into the conversation ten years earlier when they were out walking in the grounds of a local National Trust pile, the annual activity which had become their low-key acknowledgement of another year together. For Patrick, taken a little by surprise, her proposal suggested their metaphorical descent was suddenly over, the mountain replaced by a broad flat plain stretching as far as the eye could see. Thus 'downsizing' prompted him to think of something beyond the sensible and practical; it felt like giving up, as if the future ahead was going to be bland and inconsequential, as if all excitement was behind them and there was nothing else to look forward to. But knowing Kate's logic was sound - as it had seemed to be for over forty years! - he went along with the idea, and for a few weeks they toured estate agents and browsed websites looking for their final 'forever home'. But their hearts proved not to be in it, and eventually they conceded they could do without the fuss and expense of moving, and that it was useful having the extra space for when either Sarah or Henry brought their expanding families to visit - even if for just a day. So little changed. Gradually they got older, time went faster.

And ten years later, on the verge of their 'golden' anniversary?

As he contemplates tomorrow's walk, a dull pain reminds Patrick of the trouble he has been having with his knees over the last couple of years. He wants to avoid giving it a name as naming something makes it real, allows it to attach itself to you, and, once attached, means it's even more difficult to shake off. It's 'another one of those things' age bestows on you whether you want it or not: the need for an extra wee in the middle of the night, the slight shortness of breath when reaching the top of the stairs, the inability to snap open a tight jar lid the way you used to. Knowing there is nothing he can do about any of those things doesn't help. Indeed, birthdays have become less a cause for celebration and more a kind of bodily MOT where you discover that during the previous twelve months something else has worn down, seized up, or fallen off. But he will walk tomorrow all the same because Kate will want him to, even though she won't be there with him.

She was spared the gradual decline to which Patrick now finds himself subject, and occasionally he tries to find some consolation in the thought she avoided all the nonsense attendant on remorseless physical degradation. Virginia Woolf or not, she would have hated that. Of course, he has no possible conception of how the end had been for her, no notion of the terror she may have felt as the speeding car - being chased by the police - tore round the corner at the top of the High Street and mounted the pavement. There can be no doubt she would have heard the wail of the sirens behind her and, if she did, was it not likely that she would have turned to see what all the fuss was about? But in reconstructing the scene as he has been unable not to do in the intervening four years, he tells himself that she had been unaware, most likely distracted by notices in the Newsagent's window: offers of second-hand sofas; Yoga or homeopathy classes; or puppies - again! - from number thirty-two's unspayed Labrador-cross. Conscious of the crisis or not, he was told it would have been over in a flash, as if that made any difference. They were trying to be kind, consoling, yet they failed to recognise that for him it could never be over in a flash; each day for the rest of his life would be slower and emptier.

There had been an investigation, the outcome of which was to suggest failings on the part of the chasing police car: knowing they were coming up to the High Street they should have slowed down, backed off. It was a verdict which provided compensation for Patrick - as if money made any difference. When the cheque arrived he imagined Kate looking over his shoulder and joking "never mind downsizing, now you can afford to *up*size!" Needless to say, he never moved.

Smoking in the Park

"Do you mind if I smoke?"

It was a question which seemed to come to him not so much from the mouth that had uttered the words but from another point in time, almost another world. Did anyone smoke any more? Hadn't it become frowned upon and virtually outlawed, a private and discrete pastime rather than something shared or - even worse - imposed on others? But some things never change. He remembers how the question had been asked not because it was a genuine enquiry, one whose answer would determine action or inaction, but rather as a matter of convention, delivered as if offering a negative response was inconceivable. And now here he was again, reliving the whole exchange as if he was present there once more, as if the words - thanks to their travelling through time - had managed to drag him backwards, the evidence of his temporal displacement being to imagine Isaac before him with a cigarette between his fingers, lighter poised in his other hand.

Convention then, and not a real question at all.

"I thought you were giving up."

Isaac laughs.

"Where on earth did you get that notion?" He flicks the lighter and applies the consequent flame to the end of the cigarette which is now between his lips. After an initial drag, he removes it from his mouth while simultaneously burying the Zippo back in his pocket. "And as you can see, I haven't."

There had always been something in the manner of Isaac's smoking he found oddly attractive, seductive almost: the way he pursed his lips as they held the Gitanes, the delicacy bestowed on his fingers when it smouldered between them, even the way in which he would stub the cigarette out under the sole of his shoe. It was clichéd, he knew that, but even so...

"You were never tempted?" Isaac asks, as if applying the question simultaneously to two parallel conversations. It was another of his defining characteristics, this ability to say one thing and refer to another not even tangentially related.

"A long time ago." He wants to add 'as you know' but is unsure of his ground, as if there is some danger he would be making it up, falling into the trap of locating Isaac in a place he had never occupied. Trap or vicarious wish-fulfilment? "And not so much tempted either. I tried it for a while."

"Really?"

He is unsure whether Isaac's surprise is genuine.

"I thought it would make me more interesting, you know?" The way Isaac shakes his head tells him he cannot comprehend why anyone would need to do that because he cannot conceive of it for himself. "Gauloises, unfiltered. Or menthol."

"My, you were trying hard!" Isaac laughs, arcs his fingers, parts his lips, draws again.

"But it didn't work."

"In what way did it not work? You make it sound like an experiment from which there should have been concrete, definable and measurable outcomes."

Was that how it had been? He recalls how he had set out some vague benchmarks, a virtual list of things that might happen - or stop happening - should his smoking have had the desired effect. Usually these outcomes revolved around women - Caroline most of all. Is that too much to try and explain? Not only cognisant of the difficulty such a task would pose, he fails to give any credence to the need to do so given Isaac is Caroline's brother. To see if he can shake off the other man's challenge, shed himself of both the enquiry and the memory, he looks out across the gardens of Charlecote and pretends to be admiring the late daffodils, the promise of a summer yet to come. How different would this vista have been back when he was a novice smoker? He imagines it exactly the same, the people walking the paths as anonymous as those before him now.

"She sends her regards," Isaac says, puffing out a brief cloud and directing his gaze towards the long drive.

"Caroline?"

"No, the Queen." Isaac smiles without turning. There had been a joke back then that he and his family were somehow related to royalty; it had always amused him. After dropping the remains of his cigarette onto the path and crushing it under his light tan shoes, Isaac looks back at him. "Who else?"

"How is she?"

"Well enough, Seth. Considering."

The pause before Isaac's last word is sufficient to introduce many layers of complexity as if he has practiced rolling and folding and refolding it until he is able to produce the finest and most subtle word-puff-pastry in the world. A suddenly yawning chasm opens in front of Seth, a gap into which Isaac steps lightly by fishing yet another cigarette from the packet in his pocket.

A hoot on a car horn levers Seth from the calm of Charlecote and rudely deposits him back in the city centre park-side cafe where he has been sitting for some time now. Dragged from reverential immersion in the past, Seth finds himself stunned by the sudden intrusion of noise. Beyond the expanse of tables and chairs where he sits there is an ocean of green, a sea populated with a pantomime of moving people; yet this green carries the shades not of spring but of autumn, and the majority of those who punctuate the scene are neither strolling nor admiring the view, but rather travelling head down with a purpose, knowing there is somewhere else they need to be. However, it is not this human mélange which locates him most of all but rather the roar of London, a symphony playing in the background like an endless theme tune you cannot usurp from your consciousness. Irrespective of his knowing he is - as yet - alone at his table, Seth cannot help but look to his left, half-expecting to see Isaac sitting there having been simultaneously transported with him from Warwickshire all those months ago, cigarette in his lips, Zippo in mid-strike; and when he does not find him, he feels he has been robbed, as if the past has been taunting him for no good reason other than its own private pleasure.

As a slight gust of wind hits him - not cold in itself but rather one carrying an omen of the winter soon to come - he notes, as if for the first time, most of the tables are unoccupied. In front of him a cafetière sits half-full and in the cup alongside the dregs from its first pouring. Perhaps it had been the taste of coffee which had transported him to the café at Charlecote; perhaps wrapped in the green of the park there had been enough in the simple act of drinking and sitting - and in the reason for his waiting, of course! - to allow him to block out the noise and find himself back there again. After all, what better preparation could he have concocted? He closes his eyes for a moment and tries to will himself back into April, wanting to be reabsorbed into those minutes with Isaac and complete their narrative, because he knows how important that was for what will soon follow. But the sense of immediacy he had enjoyed is lost, and now all he can do is to recreate the scene artificially - and in the past tense. As if he were a key which might unlock something intangible, he tries to think of Isaac, to reimagine his physical being, his elegance, his unique ability to command the stage; but all he can conjure up is a dialogue filtered by his memory and corrupted by language. It is as if he has gone from acting in a play to merely sitting in the front row of the stalls and watching the action unfold.

"Considering?" he had said.

Isaac raised an eyebrow.

"You knew what she was going through?"

"We aren't exactly on each other's Christmas card lists any more." Seth wanted to add 'as you know' for the second time but again refrained from doing so; Isaac was the only conduit he had to a past that used to matter to him more than anything in the world. "So from that perspective I confess to being woefully out of date."

"Until when?" There was a matter-of-factness in Isaac's voice, a shift in tone Seth could hardly mistake.

"Until when what?"

"How up-to-date are you? I mean in terms of Caroline."

"Let's see…" Whether or not his exaggerated pause was interpreted by Isaac as the somewhat theatrical gesture it had undoubtedly been, Seth tried to show no concern either way. Yet he had no reason to delay. There was nothing which required time in order to be dredged up from some historical memory bank; the facts were at forefront of his mind. As ever. "We went on holiday - that disastrous trip to Tuscany - then came home. There was an argument about nothing in particular, then another, and another. I lost track of what the arguments were about given they soon blended seamlessly one into the next. And then one day Caroline was gone - to you first I think and then elsewhere. Although I was not sure what I had done wrong - indeed, if I had done anything wrong at all - I tried for reconciliation. Perhaps not hard enough. Anyway, a few months later I heard rumours about Robert or Rupert or someone. We still had a few mutual friends left at that point."

"Rupert," Isaac confirmed, needlessly.

"After that, I heard about someone else, but the voices bringing me information were increasingly few and far between. Perhaps I'd stopped listening, I don't know." Not for the first time Seth looks for a conclusion. "The last concrete fact? Something I could really hang my hat on as being true? No idea."

Seth looked at his companion as if challenging him to dispute the version of events as presented; but rather than say anything, Isaac simply nodded and, remembering his cigarette, took another drag.

Recalling the bark of a dog, Seth looks up into the London park of his present, confirms he is still alone, then pours the remainder of the coffee from the cafetière into his cup. The past plays on. Although in focus, its images possess an odd sense of the sepia about them, Isaac cast in the mould of a Thirties' matinee idol.

"She wasn't well, Seth. Tell me you knew that. Or at least suspected as much."

Seth shook his head.

"I didn't know. Honestly. I knew she was having problems at work, was getting stressed far too often. Italy was supposed to help her relax, be a bit of a safety valve. That's all I knew at the time." Seth paused. "Maybe I'd been blinded by the situation, how difficult it was. If you wanted me to I could probably go back and construct something, impose the idea of her being unwell on those last few months to see if the notion would fit…"

"You don't need to do that." Isaac dropped the latest cigarette to the ground and crushed it. The softness of such a brutal gesture surprised Seth. "None of us knew; and especially not Caroline. I think she was already part way into her breakdown before you went to Italy… She never seemed very good at expressing how she felt when things weren't going well - at least as far as I could see, and I grew up with her... You - " Isaac looked away to where a dog was barking then almost immediately back at Seth, "you were collateral damage I'm afraid. You didn't do anything wrong, at least not as far as I could make out. And as for your attempts to get her back - which would have been good not just for you but for her too as it turns out - well, thank you." Isaac lifted his packet of Gitanes from his pocket but then chooses to leave it resting on his leg. "Rupert was a mistake, of course. As was Tom soon after. But she was just bouncing around by then, careering about, not really knowing what was going on, what she was up to, what she was looking for. She had this notion that she'd lost something. Or had had something stolen from her. I don't know if she blamed anyone for that."

The pause was sufficient for Seth to feel the need to fill it.

"Me?"

"I don't know. I'm pretty sure she didn't, not really. And you need to realise that by that stage no-one was one her Christmas card list."

It was a weak joke. Seth watched Isaac's fingers as they played with the packet of cigarettes.

"We managed to get her away from that dreadful job - it had been slowly killing her - and onto some medication. Some serious medication. She lived back with our parents for a while, and for a while with me too. We took turns. It was a long haul - for us yes, but for Caroline most of all. Last year..." Isaac, with an air or resignation, picked up the Gitanes and withdrew one. Seth watched him as he repeated the steps with his fingers, his lips, the Zippo - yet this time it was as if they were being executed by a different person entirely, someone devoid of elegance and grace.

"Last year?" Seth prompted.

"Was the hardest." A drag, a puff of smoke. "For a while... Well, for a while we thought it was touch and go. But gradually she began to improve; the shutters were lifted a little; she started talking about the past - tentatively at first, but that was something. I think she was trying to cleanse herself, slowly purge the poison from her mind."

Isaac stared at his cigarette as if it held the answers for which he too was searching, as if by taking its nicotine into his lungs he would become enlightened. Seth wondered if Isaac's smoking had become the transference of his desperation into something physical.

"And then, a few weeks ago, she asked after you."

"Me?"

"Out of the blue. As if she'd worked her way through her past chronologically (either forwards or backwards) and arrived at the point where you came in - or went out, as it were. She wanted to know how you were, what you had done after she left you."

"So you said you'd find out," Seth concluded.

"Of course; isn't that what brothers are there for, to dig up the corpses of boyfriends past?"

This time the joke proved a little more robust and they both laughed.

"Hence my call. And hence my request."

"And us being here today."

"Indeed. Neutral territory." A pause. "Part one successfully navigated. I hope."

Seth checks his watch and lifts the coffee to his lips, savouring the smell before he allows the liquid into his mouth. It is nearly eleven. From behind his chair he hears footsteps and turns just as a waitress appears at his side. She pauses dutifully, all black-and-white; even her question - as to whether he needs anything else - is starkly monotone. He wants to say 'how long have you got?' and invite her to sit down so that he can share something with her, even though he is unsure exactly what that would be. Instead he asks for another cafetière and a fresh cup.

Part three requires a fresh cup.

At Charlecote he had then given Isaac a potted version of his unremarkable life post-Caroline, leaving out the unrelated, the irrelevant. Isaac's supplementary question - "has there been anyone special since then?" - he sidestepped with, he thought, such a graceful swerve that Maradona would have applauded. There had been no need to burden Isaac - and thus Caroline, presumably - with the failures of his meagre love life. Perhaps it had been that which - the natural corollary to Isaac's "what's happened to you since then?" - had provided a natural segue into part two.

"She wants to write to you," Isaac had said. It was as if he was crossing a threshold, asking permission, brokering a deal. Even though he had all the prerequisite attributes, the notion of Isaac as middleman seemed strangely incongruous. "Or rather, she wants your permission to be given a letter from her."

"Sounds odd, putting it that way."

Isaac had smiled.

"It's actually the only way I can put it given I have the letter in my pocket. She's already written it."

Seth remembers being stunned. He wants to equate that moment with the sun suddenly disappearing behind a cloud, Charlecote being sheathed in grey, a shiver passing through his body; but the statement had no such accompaniment. Isaac pulled an envelope from his pocket and allowed it to rest on his knee exactly where his cigarette packet had lain a few minutes earlier. They both looked at it.

"Not for now. Later. When you get home. Or when I've gone." The latter phrase sounded like a plea to be allowed to go, to be released.

Seth had not taken it immediately. He had asked Isaac what was in it, but Isaac didn't know. He had asked when she had written it, why she had written it - all questions for which her brother had no adequate answer, only guesses.

"I think," he said, after some consideration, "this may not be her first draft. And so I have to deduce that either she found putting pen to paper difficult or she wanted to get it right. Or both. Perhaps it's part of her healing journey."

"Of removing the poison?"

Isaac nodded, then realised the implication of his doing so.

"Not that you were poisonous in any way, Seth! I don't believe that for a moment. And I don't think Caroline does either. You know, the way she asked after you, the way she asked if I would do her this favour... I think, if nothing else, it may be a form of apology." Isaac taps the envelope. "Perhaps that's what this is."

Seth recalls a couple walking past them just at that moment, the shouts of children playing nearby, the clatter of something being dropped inside the café. Or was that just fantasy, misremembering, unnecessary embellishment? He held out his hand for the envelope, he knows that much. And he knows that Isaac took it and shook it - as if sealing the deal - before handing him the letter, saying "Thank you", and then standing and walking away. Seth remembers feeling the weight of the envelope in his hand as he watched Isaac retreat. After about fifty yards he stopped, retrieved his cigarettes and lighter from his pockets once more, then moved on again through a puff of blue smoke.

That had been the beginning of part two.

He had sat there and read Caroline's letter twice before refolding the pages and returning them to the envelope. Then he had stood, looked around as if expecting to see Isaac somewhere nearby, observing him, before heading toward the main path and the car park. Once home he read it again, and then the following day too, each time marvelling at the precision of the handwriting. Perhaps when Isaac suggested Caroline had wanted to get it right he had been closer to the truth than he realised; it wasn't just the meaning of the words that mattered but how they looked on the page. Her script had been precise, as if she hadn't wanted any unfortunate blemish to get in the way of the words - and for those initial readings Seth could not fail to be absorbed by how carefully they had been committed to the paper.

A sudden lull in the city's roar permits the sound of bells to reach him, and Seth checks his watch and then scans all the paths visible from where he sits. Eleven o'clock. And then the backing track reasserts itself. Isaac had been partially correct in his assumption that the letter might have represented an apology, not that Caroline said 'sorry' anywhere, not in as many words. But there was undeniably something *unwritten* on those three pages, hidden between the lines as if she had resorted to invisible ink for her confession. She spoke of her illness and of what had caused it; she tried to explain how she had felt, what had led her into such a dark place. Her reference to Italy was merely tangential - and any reference to leaving him non-existent. Overall however, there was something gently upbeat in her tone, as if she were forcing herself to try and see her glass at least a quarter full. She had written "once more I am beginning to recognise the face that greets me in the mirror each morning" as if that were a partial triumph; she talked of finding her old self, "a person I didn't realise I had missed". And then she had asked if he would write back, if it wasn't too much trouble, if he would do that for an old friend. She didn't want an email - "I no longer trust them" she had said, making an oblique reference to the job that had ruined her - but would prefer something more 'immediate and personal': "you have to make an effort when you put pen to paper; it's more meaningful; you leave something of yourself in the marks you make". The language she had used struck him as suffused with wisdom and pain and learning, and all the more potent as a result. So he had written - and taken more than one draft himself in order to try and do her words justice; if Caroline had striven to get it right then surely he owed her that much too.

Evidently encouraged by what he had written, she had responded promptly. Deprived of a 'Sent Items' folder, he found himself unable to recall exactly what he had said - then or now - but he too must have found a tone that was suitable. Without any agenda or motive, he wrote again. If this was helping her, well, that was the least he could do. And then, in her third letter, she had asked "Would it be impossible for me to see you again, for us to meet?" She had used the word 'closure'; yet he told himself he had already found his version of closure, that he had moved on. Doing so, Seth could only translate her version of the word into one that meant the exact opposite. He dithered for days. There was a part of him wanting to say 'no'; the Seth who was only interested in self-protection; the Seth who had managed to put the past behind him - even if he had not. Yet there was another side of him that wanted to carry on helping Caroline, because he found himself hoping that's what he had been able to do. If he could assist her in the pursuit of her own closure then wasn't that what he should do? For old time's sake?

In the end impulse triumphed and he sent her an email, naming a date and a place: a park, not one that they used to frequent. Neutral territory again. He suggested eleven o'clock. She had replied with a single word: "yes". Yet even with all the backstory, the details of Isaac's approach both perfectly and imperfectly remembered, the pages of her letters, the way her words were both plain and complex at the same time, saying one thing and yet not ruling out the unsaid - just like her brother! - even with all that, Seth sits with his coffee still not entirely sure why he is there.

An impulse forces him to turn and look away to his right. About fifty yards away Caroline walks towards him. As he watches her, simultaneously she seems someone known and a stranger. He recognises the beige coat, the dark green scarf (it had been a Christmas present one year), and there is something familiar in the way she walks which reminds him both of the Caroline he once knew and of Isaac too. Yet already he can tell she is a little older, somewhat careworn, as if the last two or three years have been harder on her than on anyone can imagine. The coat looks a size too large. She stops when she is a few feet from him and tries a smile. It is enough to make him stand - before it freezes him for a moment, paralysed and not knowing what he is supposed to do next. In spite of her nervousness, her obvious fragility, she rescues him.

"Aren't you going to invite a girl to sit down?"

"I ordered coffee," is all he can manage as she completes her advance, resting her hand briefly on his arm before sitting down.

For a moment he wonders if Isaac shouldn't be there too, and quickly scans the horizon to try and locate him.

"Have you lost someone?" She asks.

It is another question he is unable to resolve. And as he sits he wonders whether, if lost and found are on opposite sides of the same coin, they might all too easily become confused. And then she spares him the agony of trying to find an answer.

"Do you mind if I smoke?"

The Big Red Button

SAM wakes him gently, anonymously. It is just as they said it would be, like coming round from a general anaesthetic: one minute you're asleep, the next you're not. And you remember neither the sleeping nor the waking, but find yourself relaxed and calm, for a few seconds thinking nothing at all - as if you are reconnecting with yourself, waiting for something to catch-up. A re-boot.

He allows his eyes to reacquaint themselves with the environment, complete an inventory - not that anything could possibly be missing. After all, what was removable, and who could have been there to steal it anyway?

When his pallet begins to alter its angle, gradually rising to shift him into a more upright position, he looks at his left hand where two of his fingers are attached to sensors and a clear tube extends from the implanted terminal in the back of his wrist. SAM has been monitoring him since he woke up - as she has been for the last few weeks - and now probably knows him better than he knows himself. For this reason he has decided SAM can only be a 'she', even if SAM never speaks. She is the partner who has judged that his vital signs are stable and at appropriate levels to permit him to get up.

"Okay, I get it," he says to no-one. He flexes the fingers of his right hand and uses them to remove the sensors from his left; then, closing the associated valve, carefully disengages the tube. One way or another, he will be needing that again soon enough.

There are strict rules as to what he can and can't do; rules drummed into him during his short but intense training. As he prepares to stand, he looks round the small cockpit and over to where the back of the solitary chair greets him, facing away like a shy lover. Except for the one obvious thing he needs to do - the one for which he has been woken - all the other activities he has been given permission to undertake are essentially pointless. If there were any he should not attempt SAM would protect him from those anyway.

They have kept things simple. "You should run some checks", he was told, though this involves nothing more than casting his eyes over various panels to ensure all their lights are green. Ridiculous, really. He suspects if any were of another hue either SAM would have dealt with them already or - if their consequences were likely to be severe - she would never have woken him in the first place. He can see nothing but green. There are odd flashes of bright orange, switches and toggles he has been instructed not to press, pull or flick. Suspecting they will have been disabled for flight, he is immediately tempted to try one, just to check his theory; and then his training kicks in: "For at least five minutes after waking, touch nothing". He is struck by the importance of colour and the limited palette presented to him: green and orange, and everything else a kind of silvery grey, even his suit. The exceptions are the black of the chair - and the button recessed in the facia beyond, currently hidden from view. Suddenly doubting himself, he checks again that all the lights he can see *are* green. Disappointment wages a short war with relief.

He now has less than an hour to reacquaint himself with where he is, to move to the black chair, to take some readings from various dials, and then make the single decision that needs to be made - and thus subsequently take (or not take) the only concrete and meaningful action demanded of him before he returns to his pallet, plugs the tube back into his wrist and opens the valve again. Just beyond the black chair he can see a small portion of the ship's porthole, its frame appearing more silver than the rest of the cabin, enhanced by the contrast with what lies beyond. The Major told him not to look out of the window until he was ready, until he had completed his initial checks and was certain he understood where he was. "For some", the Major had said, "it can be too much". He is strangely reassured to know there is something that is still down to him, driven by his fallibility, his unpredictability, his being human. Minutes away from the ultimate demonstration of that, the realisation makes him shiver.

"Maybe a couple more minutes then," he says, suddenly grateful for the conditioning which prevented him from leaping up and heading straight to the chair and the window.

Yet he waits perhaps less than thirty seconds, lured by what he needs to see and do.

As soon as he is near the seat his eyes are inevitably drawn not to the porthole but to a recess in the sparse desk immediately in front of the chair. Inside the recess, guarded by an unbreakable perspex plate, a large button. It is red, circular, around three centimetres in diameter. In a smaller housing slightly above it, two pairs of illuminated digits, separated by a colon, glow brightly: a timer, ticking down. The first two numbers tell him that in roughly thirty-two minutes the perspex panel will slide away to expose the button; it will remain that way for fifteen seconds and then the panel will slide back into place. At that point he will either have pressed the button or he won't - in both scenarios he will then need to return to his pallet and be forced back to sleep.

He sits in the chair without taking his eyes off the button, the numbers. He watches two zeroes appear to the right, the thirty-two become thirty-one, and is struck by the inevitability of it all: the digits *will* become zeroes, the perspex *will* slide away, he *will* make a decision. Even indecision will be interpreted by SAM as him making a choice. It is a realisation which forces another shiver; or perhaps this is the result of something else, his new physical status: awake, disconnected from his tube, moving for the first time in a long while.

When he drags his eyes away from the console he can only look to the window. Although appearing black, outside it is deep blue, dark purple; a canvass punctuated by thousands of pin-pricks of light, the occasional swirl of a galaxy, the glint of a planet perhaps. He thinks of Van Gogh as if doing so will ground him, then focusses on a small cluster of stars, trying to decipher his connection to them, to see how they are moving relative to him. Appearing static, they must be too far away, glued in place across an impossible horizon. Had he been so inclined, he could have consulted SAM, attempted to fix his position and identify his interstellar companions, but there seems little point, he has more important things to do. Or one at least. Glancing down at the console again, the numbers blink back at him: twenty-eight. Where did those three minutes go?!

Time. Although he knows it is not elastic - how could he forget 'the Arrow of Time'? - it suddenly feels so: weeks passing without recognition, then the slow drag of his awakening; and now, in the blink of an eye, three minutes mislaid. He looks back at the countdown and tries to imagine the ticking sound an antique clock would make as the seconds passed, generates them in his head, mentally counting. "Seven, six, five". The arrow, straight and true. And what about the remaining minutes before the perspex slides? Fast or slow?

A second question assaults him.

On a nearby screen, SAM has displayed a list of the things he needs to accomplish between waking and sleeping. It appears a long list, but this is deceptive. Almost eighty-percent of it relates to individual checks, the lights he has already glanced over, the validation that he is still alive, his ship moving, on course. And if it were not? SAM would already have them somewhere else - and he would still be asleep, none the wiser. At the bottom of the screen the last two lines: "depress the button / do not depress the button", and "return to your pallet". Nowhere is there any instruction as to how he should reach the decision which will inform his action in that penultimate step. He thinks of the Major and back to his training - and can recall nothing there either. He is on his own.

Of course there were anecdotes from previous missions. The first traveller who pressed the button - and the first who did not - both legendary. Since then there have been so many that whoever goes next is automatically and incrementally less significant. Yet even in their insignificance each would have faced the same dilemma, the same basic choice as he; so why no guidance? "Because we are all different" he tells himself, uncertain if he has spoken out loud. "Because, no matter how you try and dress it up, it's about me and no-one else."

Twenty-four.

Volunteering had seemed the only logical thing to do. Someone had suggested it was the equivalent of 'human recycling': taking something that was at the end of its normal lifespan and giving it a second chance. Even so, it was more about the planet than him; a dying, toxic planet where each day spent living there shortened your life expectancy by two. They had seen it coming, kept quiet about it - but seen it coming none the less. Secretly funded covert missions began at the turn of the century, a prolonged attempt to find a long-term alternative to Earth. Only when they were ready, when the first volunteers had embarked and there had been enough 'error' to move beyond the status of 'trial', only then did they come clean, a global alliance of governments and businesses forged from necessity.

That had been eight years ago. Now there were hardly any disasters. Thanks to advances in 3-D printing and machines that could create materials stronger and more heat-resistant than anything occurring naturally, they had perfected a means to mass produce suitable small craft. Into precision-moulded panels those same machines could simultaneously and seamlessly integrate circuitry and computer chips. That had been the clincher, as had nuclear propulsion and the development of AI to such a level of sophistication that they could create SAM: a series of electronic pulses, bits and bytes so unnervingly powerful that they could tell when you were hungry or thirsty or tired. Or sad. The thought makes him glance over his shoulder to where he imagines SAM would be if she were a real person, standing there watching him. He wonders how she might evaluate his mood right now. He could ask, if he wanted.

The first two digits flash "21".

He was luckier than most, he knows that. Every single person on the planet had been assessed and scored against a stringent set of criteria: age, intelligence, underlying heath, skills and abilities, projected lifespan, mental stability and acuity. Rumour had it there were a hundred metrics, though he struggled to imagine how they could come up with that many. The vast majority of the global population came up short because of some negative combination of age, intelligence and health. Only a sliver of the subsequent minority made it through all the secondary measures. An ever smaller proportion of those were invited to take more tests. By the time these were whittled down even further, only a minuscule percentage was left. They were into remote decimal places.

Staring at the retreating numbers, he is somehow surprised that from 20:00 they change to 19:59 and don't go to 19:99; he feels as if he has had forty seconds stolen from him. Forty seconds in each minute as if it were a tax, or the impact of a high interest rate set against a dodgy loan.

The day he got the final results had started like any other. From his apartment he could just about make out some of the buildings across the city, the ones poking their heads above the smog-cloud. And he knew it would be hot outside; so hot that even his air-conditioned car would offer little respite as he took his turn to go into the office. When the message came through, all the personal devices in his flat bleeped or flashed simultaneously: his watch, his headphones, his FitCom. Out of habit he searched for his phone.

YOU HAVE BEEN OFFERED THE OPPORTUNITY TO VOLUNTEER. PLEASE REPLY 'YES' OR 'NO'. YOU HAVE 24:00:00.

As soon as he opened the message the countdown started. The first countdown. During those initial few minutes he kept checking his phone, his watch; was that to verify he'd had the message in the first place or to watch the time ticking away? At the last set of tests he'd attended, the candidates had been advised not to agonise over their decision. "Inside you know what you really want to do. So go with your gut; it won't be wrong." As he looked at the message during that first hour he discovered his gut had gone walkabout.

When he eventually got to the office he found himself on edge, wondering if the news of his offer had leaked out somehow - or worrying that he might be making his good fortune all too evident. And it *was* seen as good fortune. He was to be envied; that was the popular view. There had been colleagues who couldn't wait to share their news; in many cases they simply became unbearable, working with them during their final two weeks difficult and frustrating. He had promised himself he would tell no-one. No-one.

Having set that precedent sometime earlier, he had made further excuses to Jen. When he'd first had to go off for two days of tests he told her it was because of a project at work - luckily believable given he was a construction engineer of sorts. So when they needed him for a final week training - once he had replied 'YES' to that message - it simply became the culmination of the fictitious project; the client needed him on-site. Which in a way was true.

It had taken him until lunchtime to make up his mind, and it hadn't been his gut that made the call as much as the circumstances of the day: the slow drive; the heat; the security checks; the medication; the monotony of the office. He felt bored and unfulfilled; he could imagine no future, nothing to look forward to. It was a little before one when he pulled out his phone, typed 'YES', and hit 'Reply'. Only after that did he think of Jen.

Of course he loved her. He had never questioned that. But weren't they just going through the motions, kidding themselves that they had something positive ahead of them? They could get married, but what difference would that make? There had been a time, long ago, when doing so was the first step towards a family, building the next generation; but all of that had morphed into legend for everyone except the elite. Unless you lived in one of the Secure Zones - cleansed, anaesthetised, sterile - you couldn't have children, they simply didn't survive. How could they if being alive for one day cost you two days of living? The population had been shrinking for decades now. There were no longer any children under the age of seven. Marriage - like work - what was the point?

16:47

Was it cowardly that when he left on the final morning - not for work, but for the Space Centre - he still hadn't told her? Cowardly that he had arranged for her to receive a message from him at the end of a day when he knew it would be too late to change anything, when he would already be away, somewhere above the stratosphere hurtling through space? Even though he knew any such message would be inadequate, he had spent days wording and rewording it. He tried to play up the possibility that she might be one of the next ones chosen, that she would one day join him and they could still build the future they both wanted. After all, wasn't his mission 'Plan A'? That's what they'd told him. And if it were 'Plan A', then surely they'd want to get as many people engaged in it as possible. Jen was a good candidate. Having seen some of the people who'd made it through to final training, he was certain of that. Perhaps they were there because of specialist technical skills - he knew that scored highly - but surely there was nothing materially deficient in Jen.

Later however - when there was no going back - he began to question whether his wasn't 'Plan A' at all, but 'Plan B'? A last desperate throw of the dice? What if the Secure Zones were really 'Plan A', and the only feasible outcome was a future where the planet was inhabited in bio-domes, and outside there were gradually no ten-year-olds, no teenagers, no people under thirty, no people at all? But that wasn't what he had been told.

They had discovered the planet on the edge of the Solar System. When they called it "a Class M planet" he felt as if he were an extra in some ancient and legendary sci-fi TV series. For years they had assumed there could be no such place, nothing akin to Earth; and then one-day, there it was, accidentally discovered by an almost forgotten probe destined for somewhere else entirely. Real needle-in-a-haystack territory. The first people they sent had been the true pioneers, their names carved into the entrance hall wall at the Space Centre. Two groups of six sent into the vast reaches; almost literally a wing and a prayer. Nearly three years later, the first messages returned, their initial words as much ingrained into popular culture as Neil Armstrong's "giant leap" had been over a century before:

ARRIVED. TIRED BUT FIT. TEMPERATE HERE. BETTER THAN WE COULD HAVE HOPED FOR. SUNSETS BRILLIANT.

The final two words had been grasped by the masses in the same way a thirsty man might clutch at a cup of water. Few people on Earth could remember brilliant sunsets. Some people - the doubters, the sceptics, the doom-mongers - thought the messages were phoney. Most other people just wanted the chance to go and see for themselves, the chance he had now been given.

He could record a message for Jen here and now. All he would have to do would be to ask SAM and the camera would roll, a few days later the package arriving unexpectedly in her email like spam. She might delete it unread. Perhaps it would be sent from the Administration; if so, she'd have no choice but to open it. But what could he now say that would make any difference? How could he adequately explain, especially when he wasn't as sure of the facts - or of himself - as he might wish to be?

13:15

There was another option. An option thirteen minutes away.

He could go back.

One of the lessons the Administration learned from the first few flights was that, once they were on their way, some of the pioneers suddenly realised they'd made a huge mistake and taken the wrong decision. Their gut had failed them. But it had been too late; they were 'all in'. Most had adjusted, either on the flight or once they reached their destination, and excitement - or the sunsets! - got the better of them. But there was one case in those early days of expensive, multi-occupancy ships, where the individual concerned - known historically as Crew Member G092 - had simply lost it, having to be incarcerated in transit and on arrival. Or at least that was the story. Rumours suggested a somewhat more binary end.

So later they added 'The Big Red Button' into the console of the single-person vessel, the one-off chance to abort. Hence the sliding back of the perspex panel and the fifteen seconds during which it was exposed. Press it, return to the pallet, plug yourself back in, and SAM would do the rest. The next thing you knew, you would be a couple of hours from Earth re-entry.

Lou Myers had been the first person to exercise that option. It made him a celebrity overnight; everyone wanted a slice of him. He may have only lived for another twelve years, but he did so totally in the limelight, feted by the media, his story examined and dissected, his reasoning probed and challenged. It was a great story for the Administration too, as much a vindication of their approach - and their humanity - as a successful landing millions of miles away. After Lou? He knew of about ten others, men and women who became lost in increasing obscurity. There were probably more. The authorities ceased to be interested in them; they had no value, hence their numbers and outcomes were generally vague. A few struggled, dying younger than they should have; busted flushes because of two bad draws. Like Stacey DiMarco who, on her return, became convinced she had made a *second* tragic mistake and lost her faculties completely. Eventually she was shot by police as she tried to storm the Space Centre armed with a couple of automatic weapons apparently determined to get another ride out of town. That was her third misjudgement. During the training they told you about Lou Myers - deliberately de-romanticising his story - and Stacey DiMarco - deliberately emphasising hers. Then that was that. You were on your own.

And of course he was, literally so. In about ten minutes he would face the same dilemma Lou, Stacey, and all the nameless others had; hundreds of people of all races and creeds, ninety-nine-plus percent of whom had watched the perspex slide back, left the button untouched, and simply carried on to the New World.

It was a big call, either way. Determined to do it justice, he realised with a chill that most of his time had already vanished, the :00 ticking over to :59 once again. He glanced out of the window as if the answer might lay there. It was an unchanged image - or rather one that had changed imperceptibly. There were the same clusters of stars he had focussed on just a few minutes previously, but now they seemed unimportant. From somewhere he dredged up an echo of the excitement he had felt when he received the original message, when he made his decision. There had been an air of bravado and comradeship during the training; the sense that they were doing something extraordinary - and not just for themselves - was palpable. All of that counted, surely? The Administration had given him an insight into what would be expected of him: the things that needed to be built or fixed; the projects he would be involved in; the expectations of him as a member of the new community, a community that had to become self-sufficient, progressive, growing. "You are the future" was one of their favourite strap-lines.

But if that was the case, if he *was* the future, did that mean everyone else, all those who could not travel, who would be left behind, were the past? Had they been given up on already? Was Jen already seen as history, one of the billions to be sacrificed? If so, then pressing the button would be equivalent to consigning himself to living out the rest of his life - a shortened life - as a time-limited non-entity with no prospects and no value. Was that what he wanted?

From his top pocket he pulled the photograph of Jen he'd put there the very first day they'd given him his suit. Placing it on the console, she smiled back at him, radiant in t-shirt and shorts, their bright colours at odds with her surroundings and the sky. It had been their day off and they had taken a trip out of the city to one of the nearby natural relics. Now little more than a misshapen crater hosting a shallow pool of fetid water, it had once been a huge lake, blue and vibrant, filled with the sort of fish you could now only see at the National Aquarium. And there, where Jen leant against a low wall, a noticeboard told the history of the lake including an artist's impression of how it might have once looked. Few people visited now, but he recalls how they'd gladly sacrificed a day just to get out and away, to be alone, to kid themselves that they could be happy and that a different kind of normal was possible.

5:31

"We can't save everyone". That had been another of their mantras, a litany of soundbites they continually employed to drive the message home. They were telling him that he was special, privileged, lucky; that he had an opportunity not only to save himself, but to do something for the good of the many. One of his co-trainees said they had been 'pulled from the dustbin': "The world's doomed along with everyone on it, so there's no choice, right?" It had been a common sentiment. He had wondered how many in his cohort had been attached; how many, on their journey through the stars, would have been able to do what he had done, pulled a photograph of someone they loved from their pocket and place it on the console in front of them. He suspected not many. The Administration didn't like to split up married couples; in their eyes you were either married or you weren't - hence, he wasn't. It was simpler that way.

But it wasn't just about bald time or longevity, was it? It was about the quality of that time too; where you spent it, who you spent it with. Without doubt - well almost certainly without doubt - he would be getting more time, a longer life; he would be busy, excited, challenged; he would be making a difference, building a legacy. Or was that the training talking? Yet he would be doing it on his own - or without Jen. There were stories, subtle ones fed into training sessions, about the pioneers who had become couples. It was something the Administration encouraged because the colonies would need to establish a future generation quickly. During training he had seen two or three pairs tentatively beginning to form, marked a look, the brush of hands. In time, that would be celebrated too. All of which suggested he might find himself in a new relationship at some point; that he might be able to fulfil all those dreams he and Jen had shared - but he would be doing so without her.

The Fairly Tale notion he had floated in the note he left her - that one day she might be able to join him so they could carry on where they had left off - felt suddenly cheap and hollow. Wasn't it more likely that within a year he would have found someone else, been drawn into a new relationship through the adventure of it all? Or through peer pressure. And the Administration. Carrying on meant extending his own life and ending Jen's; that was how it suddenly seemed. He felt like a murderer.

And still she smiled back at him from the edge of the wasted lake.

He only realised he had been crying when SAM roused him with an intermittent alarm, soft yet insistent. Looking up from where he had hung his head and closed his eyes, the countdown blinked 01:55 back at him. Then 01:54, 01:53.

Was it time? Already?

Sitting up, he tried to rouse himself mentally, adjust his posture; this was no time to be slouching or half-hearted. Jen was still there, her smile unchanged, the message in her eyes as unswerving as it had always been. And as if she could see him, he smiled back. Then he focussed on the clock, watching the numbers as they transformed through their hypnotic dance. As the one-forties morphed into the one-thirties he tried to recall all those things he had thought and felt during the past half-hour or so, like replaying a movie on fast-forward: the day he had the news, the training sessions, the day he left, the day he woke up.

Today.

And today was the day he would go back to sleep too. Unless.

Whether he pressed the button or not, SAM couldn't force him back into the cot; couldn't force him to plug himself back in, to ready himself for her soporific drugs. He could just sit there and do nothing, watch the stars go by. He could choose to get tired on his own terms, to fade away. Or to plug himself back in much later - perhaps when it was too late.

It was another choice to be made, one no-one had ever spoken of or warned them about. But it was a choice nonetheless; another opportunity for him to assert his humanity.

The tone of SAM's alarm changed as the first two digits harmonised to zeroes. He felt his heart racing, his breath shortening. He watched the third digit change from a three to a two, and then…

Five seconds later the perspex panel slid silently away. Naked before him, the red button. Voices in his head telling him to press it - to not press it.

As the countdown reached seven, six, five, his hand hovered. He looked again at the photograph.

Decision time.

Hope

"Why do they call you 'Chubby'?".

He glanced down to where his limp and underemployed penis lay hidden by the light duvet, then looked back to her, eyebrow raised.

"No, really. Tell me."

His attempt at a visual joke failing, hers became an inauspicious question. He would have hoped for something more, something to indicate he hadn't just experienced yet another inconsequential one-night-stand. Indeed, if that was the case then the excitement was already all over, all promise dissipated.

"And what is it with men and nicknames anyway? Your two friends last night - 'DJ' and 'Spandau' - what's that all about?"

Although she had looked outstandingly pretty the previous evening, the cold light of a new day saw plainness getting the upper hand. The usual combination of enhancements had been responsible for her elevation in his eyes: the drink, the party atmosphere, the music, the dancing. A typical birthday night-out for Spandau. Almost certainly it had been a cocktail which had transformed him for her too, and now, the morning after, she was laying a sight distance away from him with similar thoughts probably running through her head. He tired to ignore the space between them and focus on her questions.

"Well, it's DJ because those are his initials: David James. His christian names. And Spandau because when he was younger he looked a bit like the guy who was their lead singer."

"Tony Hadley."

"You know them?"

"Who doesn't? But he doesn't look a bit like Tony Hadley."

"Maybe not now. But back then he did. Before he got older. Anyway, the name stuck. It's funny."

He wasn't sure if he meant the nickname was amusing or - years later - it was bizarre that they were still using it. Perhaps doing so said more about how they were in their mid-thirties, attempting to cling to past selves.

"And Chubby?"

"That?" He smiled as one tends too when reflecting on happier times. "I used to eat like a horse and never put any weight on. For a while I had this amazing metabolism. Then one day someone said they were stunned that, considering everything I ate, I wasn't chubby. It was like a christening, and no-one let it go. Let's face it, it's slightly more interesting than Rob…"

He paused to allow her to comment; another opportunity to say something positive, to rescue a shred of potential from their shared night, the suggestion that it was still possible there could be another.

"I have to be more careful now, weight-wise." When she remained silent he had to say something. "And don't girls do nicknames in the same way?"

Again she said nothing. Half an hour later, over breakfast, the cooling embers had turned to cold cinders.

After she had gone - the harsh finality of her departure belying her soft words of farewell - Rob found himself once again contemplating an empty life. Fanciful it may have been, but he imagined himself reading a crumpled data sheet on 'Living', one given to him as a teenage birthday present from an anonymous donor - and only recently rescued from the waste basket. Akin to its medical equivalents, the sheet was filled with instructions as to what he should and should not do: '*__do not__*' was repeated far too often, the words picked out in bold italics to make sure he didn't miss them.

Warnings of side effects were couched in language which tried to play down likelihood and severity - 'one in ten thousand', 'one in five hundred' - but to him they read like a litany of all he had been through. Side effects? He'd had them all.

The predominant topic on the sheet focussed on relationships, its words telling him what to look out for and what to avoid. He imagined himself scanning bullet points only to discover he had lived his life completely the wrong way round, doing what he shouldn't have done and vice versa. "Avoid partners" it said, endeavouring to be modern and gender neutral, "who are dominant, passive, aggressive, passive-aggressive, untrustworthy, needy, disingenuous or disloyal". When he thought back to Di and Maisie and Florence, he found that, one way or another, he was able to tick every box. And it felt like looking through a one-way mirror from the side of concealment: he could see out, but was unable to cross-reference those same characteristics against himself. How would he have fared had he been able to do so? Others would have had their own view - particularly Di.

"Divorce" - the sheet told him - "was the most serious potential side effect of marriage, afflicting around one in three." Tick. So where was the advice that said in order to be assured of avoiding the pain associated with that fall-out, one should not marry in the first place? *That* would have been advice worth heeding. Towards the end, Di had clearly demonstrated her own regret, and had not been slow to complain about him. "I don't know why I married you in the first place" had been her lowest blow. Given the luxury of both hindsight and the jaundiced view into which he had all too readily settled, Rob ascribed her poor judgement not to any failings on his part but to her not reading her own 'Life instruction sheet'. "Boom!" - as Spandau liked to say.

"Be wary of making emotional commitments when either you or a potential partner are emerging from a recently failed relationship (colloquially known as being 'on the rebound')." Tick. Twice. First with Maisie who, in getting over a traumatic separation of her own, needed a shoulder on which she could initially cry and later implode. Post-Maisie, in the case of Florence it was Rob who had been in a tailspin - which made him easy meat for a woman whose sole aim in life seemed to be to milk her men dry emotionally and then move on. It had been a brief but predatorial affair, sufficient to give him a good kicking when he was already down. His data sheet offered no statistics in relation to these calamities however; there was no "one in x" warning to administer a sobering jolt designed to prevent nascent victims falling into the trap likely to open up before them. Rob wondered how such a warning might have been articulated, and what it might have scored: nine in ten? A racing certainty then. As if to offer an excuse himself, he reminded himself that he hadn't come across the idea of the data sheet until it was too late. Perhaps that was the irony of it; the sheet played back the cumulative results of an experiment called 'living', results only relevant *after* the event - as if it were a belated conscience, 'lessons learned' in italics and boldface.

DJ and Spandau had tried to help him through these dark passages, though often their clumsy attempts at resurrection left him worse off than before. The previous evening had been a case in point. Whenever Spandau started a sentence with "There's this girl..." Rob knew he should run for cover. But in this instance it had been his friend's birthday so he had no viable reason to absent himself from the party - nor avoid the introduction when it came. That she had been unusually pretty helped - as did the effects of the three G&Ts he'd already had before he met her. Their mutual spark - however it had been manufactured - proved enough to see them together at the end of the evening followed by a return to Rob's house in order to indulge in a little vacuous coupling before the following morning's denouement. Once sobered up, Rob had known Spandau would call him later in the day to see how things had turned out. Rob suspected his friend would regard the outcome as a success.

Perhaps it was inevitable Rob regarded his own suffering as being sufficiently awful to eclipse everyone else's. Wasn't that how people worked? Surely his emotional pain and current loneliness couldn't be surpassed. Wasn't the distance between himself and what he wanted - love, companionship, security - now wider than ever? He wanted someone to offer him a glimmer of hope - either that or a section at the foot of his data sheet to finally reveal the magic words which would unlock life's greatest secrets.

However, the next word he encountered proved to be nothing more remarkable than his name.

"Rob?"

Unable to say how far removed he was from that mythical paragraph he so desired, it was a familiar voice which roused him from all that was left of his reverie.

"Di."

There was a pause.

"You sound surprised," she said, trying to make light of her call, as if it were the most natural thing in the world, as if they had spoken only recently.

"I am," he replied. "How long has it been?"

"It depends how you want to measure it." Another pause. "How are you?"

"Come on Di, you didn't call to enquire after my health."

"Am I not allowed to?"

"It's just not you - not after all this time." Having answered his own question, he waited for qualification from her, but none was immediately forthcoming. "So, what do you want?"

"That's not very friendly," she bristled. "How do you know I want something?"

"Okay, okay." He tried to soften his tone, to pretend he was speaking to an old friend - which in a way he was, of course. "I'm fine, Di. And how are you? How are things in leafy Surrey?"

"Less leafy than they were."

She was not to be taken literally, he knew that. The time which now separated them had allowed him to grow a frail layer of protective skin over the wound she had inflicted on him - a wound which suddenly began to throb a little. Not only could he hear the anxiety in her voice but he could feel it inside him. She was trouble in search of a name.

"It's Charlie."

So it had a name, after all; and it was probably the name with which he would have chosen to christen it. Charles Thompson. The man she had left him for; the man who oozed smoothness and smelled like deception. Rob had tried more than once to divert her from her course. "Leave me if you want to," he had said in an increasingly rare moment of generosity, "but not for him. For yourself." She laughed at the offer - which was enough for him to stop trying to protect her, the last vestige of their love having bled away.

"You surprise me," he said, unable to restrain himself.

"That's hardly helpful," she replied, immediately picking up on his 'told-you-so' tone.

"So it's help you need then?"

She ignored the barb.

"He's left me, Rob. High and dry - and in ways you wouldn't imagine."

"Oh, I don't know," he said. "I'm only surprised it took him this long to jump ship."

"That's too cruel."

He replayed the phrase in his head.

"I didn't mean because of you. Of course not. But because of him; because he was always going to."

"You never liked him did you?" she asked.

"As far as I'm concerned, 'like' and 'Charles Thompson' are words that should never make it into the same sentence."

In the pause that followed, he imagined her looking at the cards she held; it was a weak hand, denuded of all those powerful trumps on which she used to rely. He sensed they were all played out, leaving her with a few low value clubs and diamonds; certainly nothing strong enough to take the next trick.

"I need some advice, Rob, that's all. And I don't know who else to turn to."

"Advice you'll actually listen to, you mean? For once in your life?" Whether or not he had meant to twist the knife he couldn't say. If Charlie had been responsible for the stabbing, Di was now seeking a healer - not someone to press the blade home further.

"Can you come over?"

She inhabited the house with a strange professionalism, as if her living there had nothing to do with love. When he saw her standing under the small porch, waiting, he thought she looked more like a curator than anything else - which implied he was a visitor come to see the exhibits. Not that he was surprised in the slightest. Charles always insisted in doing things on his own terms, a fact which -

considering Di's strength of personality - made it an unusual match from the outset. Perhaps she had become tired of being the dominant one in her relationship with him, and the chance to be subdued, even bullied, might have held some bizarre appeal for her. In its own way, the house was an embodiment of her allegedly departed significant other. It was all facade. The faux skin of mock Tudor frontage screamed geometry rather than whispering subtle inexactitude; the lawns were manicured rather than mowed; the path up to the house was polished rather than swept. Everywhere Rob looked, statements of wealth and attainment stared back at him; it was as if he had arrived at a physical manifestation of Charles Thompson's self-esteem. And did that include Di? Parking a little way from the front door - far enough up the drive to give himself the luxury of a few moments on the walk up to the house to compose himself - he guessed it had. In the beginning at least. Knowing the kind of man he was, how could Charles not have regarded her as a trophy? Curator she may have looked, donned in her suburban uniform, undertaking her public duties for all to see, but Rob would have been only slightly more surprised to have found her head mounted on the hall wall.

Still in motion three metres from the front door, Rob was momentarily seized by a brief panic as to how he should greet his ex-wife. Options flashed before him, each one disqualified in turn by either the passage of time or the manner in which they had parted, their final contact reliant on either email or the intermediation of their respective solicitors. Whether the same issue was facing Di or not, she resolved Rob's dilemma by turning on her heels and wordlessly leading him into the hall where she paused just long enough to close the door behind him.

"It's good to see you," she said as she walked toward and through the door immediately to her right.

Was it? Rob was, as yet, unable to pass judgement. He followed her into a sitting room which, though somewhat smaller than he had imagined it would be, betrayed in the style of sofas and soft furnishings traces of the cottage-like design she favoured. Charles had given her some leeway then. Sitting in the centre of one of the pale green settees, Di angled her body in such as way as to make it plain which of the remaining seats - both single armchairs - she expected him to take.

"So," he said, somehow obliged to open the bowling as if he had lost the toss, "how are you?"

It was a vacuous question she swatted away by simply ignoring it. Four runs. During the ensuing pause - required, Rob assumed, for her to gather her thoughts - he could not help but notice how she seemed to have matured. It was not that she looked any older than she should have - after all, three years was unlikely to make that much of a difference - but rather she gave the impression of being someone who had recently lived a more concentrated life, as if there had been little respite, no time to put up her metaphorical feet. It was, he supposed, evidence of why he was there.

"I won't waste too much of your time," she said, as if that permitted her to bypass all domestic pleasantries such as the offer of coffee. Rob wondered how distasteful the situation was for her, finding herself in such a desperate position that she had to stoop to endure his company once again. Like him, she had surely assumed once cheques were written and cashed, and legal bills paid, that would have been the end of them.

"It's Charlie," she began, the inevitable opening to a précis of her predicament. He wondered if that was all she needed to say, his name sufficient to summarise every possible negative scenario. "Two weeks ago, somewhat out of the blue, he announced he was leaving and walked out. I had been out shopping, which - as it turned out -

gave him all the time he needed to pack his bags and make his arrangements."

"Where did he go?"

"Cyprus, apparently. Said he needed to get away from me, that I had driven him out. Me!" She left the notion hanging in mid-air for a moment, chance enough to allow Rob to register how incredible the idea was. "Of course he wasn't going alone."

"Did he tell you that?"

"He's not that stupid!" The way Di made her remark Rob couldn't help but feel she was drawing a comparison with him. She pushed on. "I found out a couple of days later through a mutual friend - though I say 'friend' with some reservations… Apparently he'd been seeing someone from work for a few months. This was no sudden whim, Rob; Charlie doesn't do whims. He'd been planning it."

"You had no suspicions?" Although he knew it wouldn't advance the dialogue, it seemed the obvious question to ask.

"Oh, I always had my suspicions!" she said with distaste. "From quite early on. You know Charlie…" She paused. "Well, you don't, obviously; but you know what I mean. You could see what sort of man he was."

He avoided falling into the 'I told you so' trap, choosing not to replay a card that had already been shown.

"But isn't that good riddance then?" He settled on trying a positive spin.

At this she stood up and walked to the window, trailing her fingers along the back of the sofa as she did so.

"You'd think. And on one level it is, I suppose. But a couple of days ago I had a call from his slimy best-pal solicitor who informed me that I had just under two weeks to get out of the house; that Charlie didn't expect to find me or my things here when he got back."

"But surely he can't do that? He was the one who walked out, after all."

Di glanced back over her shoulder then returned her gaze to the garden.

"Well he can apparently - especially if you've signed a kind of prenuptial agreement that waives away just about all your rights…"

"You signed a prenup?" It was a question impossible to deliver without nuance. Di turned to face him.

"Yes, I did Rob." Her tone was defiant. "Oh, you can tell me I was an idiot to do so, but I was in a spin at the time." Something in her manner challenged Rob to deny her. She had her rebuff at the ready: that her previous decline had all been because of *him*. Rob kept his counsel. "I thought Charlie was the answer to my prayers; I though he'd give me everything I could possibly want or need, all that I'd been missing." Momentarily her chin edged a little higher. "And for a while it seemed true enough. We had parties, holidays. And I mean, look at the house."

Rob *had* looked at the house, and - whatever he might think of her now - it didn't fit the Di he had once fallen in love with. Neither did her vindictive tone. But she was on the ropes (a situation he knew well) and people were prone to out-of-character actions when desperate. He thought of Florence, and then of the recent Spandau-engineered one-night entanglement. Realising there was no way he could like the Di he was faced with at that precise moment, he glanced away from her, allowing his eyes to take in the rest of the room and its the somehow clumsy application of chintz and china, pastel and floral. A part of him knew that the most appropriate course of action was to confess sympathy and then get up and walk out; she had, after all, made her bed… But he was stopped by something dredged up from too far back to remember clearly, history encroaching on common sense. He noticed some kind of certificate framed on the far wall - too far away to read - and found himself engaging again with his imaginary data sheet; what would it have said about situations such as this?

"So what are you going to do now? Where will you go?"

In response she had said "it's just me and a few clothes, Chubby; only for a few days until I find my feet. The back room will be fine."

He had tried to resist, but the combination of Di's desperation and some residual fellow-feeling - in spite of the tone she had struck with him - painted him into a corner from which there had been no escape. They had agreed a week in order to get things sorted at their respective ends: Rob to prepare one space, and Di to ready herself to vacate another. As he drove away from what was clearly 'Charlie's house', he had recognised that "a few days" was as an imprecise a measure of time as it was possible to define. His back room - *their* old back room - was to become the staging post from which Di would prepare to relaunch herself, though he had no idea how she was going to achieve such a feat nor where she would aim. And he knew her occupation couldn't simply be confined to the back room; she would have the run of the house - her old house. He feared it would feel as if he had been invaded.

It proved more infiltration than invasion, as if the government of his life had been undermined by an outsider with questionable intent. She was no spy - indeed, there was nothing to spy on! - but she became increasingly central to how their domestic arrangements operated. Her initial offer - to "do my fair share" - had been in and of itself unremarkable. Why should she not suggest a rota for cooking and cleaning, siting his accommodation of her as a favour which required some form of repayment? The claim that she didn't want to 'put him out', although apparently delivered with sincerity, was an ambition upon which it was impossible to deliver; as soon as she walked through the door, as soon as Rob helped unload her car and carry her cases up to her designated room, it was inevitable that he was being 'put out'. And yet in spite of his doubts, the initial days progressed smoothly and harmoniously enough. By the end of the first week a new pattern had emerged, and Rob found himself beginning to make assumptions, take things for granted, place reliance on Di doing - or not doing - certain things. Indeed, a part of him relaxed into the arrangement more than he had anticipated - though he only recognised this as he cradled a whisky at the end of one evening after she had excused herself for the night. When Rob recalled their distant and more intimate past, he tried to bat such reminiscences away as irrelevant and juvenile.

"What do you mean 'it's working'?"

DJ had been incredulous when debriefed by Rob just over a week after Di's arrival. They were sitting in the bar of DJ's golf club, not because they had just finished playing, but because it was a quiet and convenient place to meet.

"How can it possibly 'work'?"

"I don't know," Rob confessed, his tone exposing a reluctance to face too much cross-examination. "We're just rubbing along okay. She's been pleasant enough; we have a routine... I had expected - what? - friction, conflict. I thought she might take over, somehow; but it hasn't been like that at all."

"She's taking advantage of you, Chubby."

"Perhaps a little. And just maybe I'm taking advantage of her too. I don't have to cook for myself every day; we share the chores; occasionally there are some nice moments..."

"You should get married," DJ said caustically. "Oh, wait. Yes, of course, you tried that."

"Very funny." Neither of them laughed.

"So when is she leaving?"

"Leaving?"

"Well, I thought it was until she found her feet or some such; until she had a better offer." DJ emptied his glass.

"It's not that easy. She's looking for work, that's the first step; trying to get back in with that recruitment agency she worked at before." Rob had been prepared for the question. "She had been able to rely on Charlie's mega-income, but now that's vanished. Maybe he's giving her money, I don't know; it's not my business. But work; everything starts from there, doesn't it? I mean, how can she move anywhere until she knows where she's working?"

"And that agency's where, exactly?"

"In town."

Wanting to say something else, DJ thought better of it and simply nodded, then glanced down at the table.

"Empty glasses." DJ paused, not moving. "Just don't forget why you two split up in the first place."

It proved to be a phrase which nagged at him throughout his journey home; even without DJ there to debate semantics, Rob was adamant they had not 'split up'. Such a phrase suggested a mutuality of decision-making where there had been none. Di had left him; it had been her decision, her choice, her reasons. Hadn't he been perfectly happy to carry on? If she hadn't had her head turned by Charles bloody Thompson wouldn't they still have been together, the back room still just that rather than what it had now become? At the time she had given him reasons, of course she had, yet he was sure these had been nothing but excuses manufactured to smooth her passage out of their relationship. He had never believed her when she told him she'd no idea why she'd married him in the first place; she had done so for the same reasons he had married her. But love - he now knew - was entirely mutable. And when had he stopped loving her? That was perhaps the biggest question of all. Catalyst or not, Charles had started a chain reaction that surged through her and into him; it had eaten away at the bedrock of what they felt for each other, and in doing so demonstrated that his foundations were the more substantial. Yet in the end even these gave way too. Was there a point of collapse? Could Rob identify a moment when love had finally seeped away through the cracks? Perhaps his saying "leave me if you want to, but not for him" was the moment he finally gave up any vestige of hope.

And perhaps in the end it was all about hope as much as anything else; as much as love, even. He let her go; he stopped fighting for *them* when he lost hope. Since those dark days it was not love his life had been lacking as much as hope. With Florence and Maisie there had been love; impure, physical, slightly deformed perhaps, but a sliver, however limited. He could see what had been missing in both those relationships had been hope, that rare emotion which - perhaps above all else - shapes a vision for the future, like peg upon which to hang a coat. Without it, love simply falls into a heap on the floor. Maisie had been too self-centred to recognise the need for anything other than that which would keep her neuroses fed. Hope, requiring at least partial investment in another person, had no place in her lexicon. It was entirely possible that Florence possessed capacity for mutuality, but by the time he met her Rob had been too desperate to recognise his need for anything beyond what he chose to call 'love', even if it was just a chimera.

"Don't forget why you two split up." As he got out of his car, Rob found himself wanting to invert the sentiment: "Don't forget why you two got together". He wondered if doing so might have been conforming to an emotional law of some kind, akin to the idea of 'an equal and opposite reaction'. It seemed, suddenly, a logical question to ask; something to ensure the rounded view. It was a conundrum for which there could be no external solution. His data sheet was only interested in consequences, not causes; cure not prevention. And even then, not really cure. But what was the point in looking back, to try and decipher the past, unless it was to inform the future? Did he know what he wanted? More recently he had thought so - a belief that gifted him Maisie and Florence. And he assumed Di had inhabited a similar space too; for that she had been rewarded with Charles Thompson, a mock-Tudor frontage, and now his own back room. *Her* old back room. Were the two of them so different after all?

Sighing, he pulled his keys from his pocket, pressed the remote to lock the car, then opened his front door. Stepping into the hall he caught the tell-tale aroma of dinner already being cooked, heard the faint sound of Di singing in accompaniment to the radio. It was like stepping into a time warp, though into the past or the future Rob could not tell.

Ursula

My father was a romantic. He used to believe everything he read in novels or saw in the movies, as if he was reading about or watching real people, and all their joy or suffering or love was real joy, real suffering, real love. Sometimes that could be charming, the most wonderful thing about him; but more often than not it wasn't. I think that's why mother had been planning to leave him, because she couldn't stand living in his world anymore, a world he thought was Fairy Tale.

That's where he got my name: books and film. D.H.Lawrence and James Bond. Well, not Bond exactly but rather from the actress who played the 'Bond girl' in *Dr. No*, the first Bond film they ever made. He loved the Bond movies. When they came out on DVD he bought them right away, paying over the odds. From then on they always seemed to be playing on the small tv in the little room he liked to call 'The Snug'. Given the room was too small for dining (its supposed purpose), christening it 'The Snug' was romantic too I suppose. I swear you could have turned the sound right down and he would have been able to provide you with the entire dialogue. I think he gave me my name because he wanted me to turn out glamorous and beautiful like that actress, or artistic and spirited like that woman from Lawrence. I think he thought names could do that to people, shape who they became. I suspect, had he lived to see what I've actually become, I'd be something of a disappointment to him. For a start I don't have Ursula Andress' looks. My body is devoid of the curves of which she could boast, and my hair isn't long and golden - though whether the colour of her hair was natural or just a component of her public persona I've no idea. And I don't have her come-to-bed eyes nor a mouth that looks as if it could suck you to death. Need I go on? Where Honey Ryder was bends and undulations, this Ursula is much more up-and-down with the odd lump in the road here and there. Not that I mind. Not really. My not living up to some goddess-template hasn't stood in the way of love or affection - though I might have had to work a little harder at getting it.

And artistic and spirited? I guess it depends how you want to measure that. For example, I can fly off the handle with the best of them, especially during my periods. Does that make me spirited? I once told an old boss what he could do with his job after he refused a holiday request and insisted I work ten straight days because the company had a big order it needed to get out. Him calling me a 'raving Commie' as a result felt like something of a triumph; I'd made my mark, stood out from the crowd. But was that brave or stupid? I didn't work for a little while after that...

To be honest I prefer a quiet, unobtrusive life. Some people might regard that as - I don't know - unambitious or passive; perhaps that's what stops me from considering myself spirited or artistic, because it isn't all about talent. At school I found I could draw pretty well; my teachers persuaded me to take A-level Art because they thought they'd unearthed a seam of some kind, a little precious metal that would make my fortune. As it turned out I was fine all the time they were telling me what to do, but when it came to working on my own, using my imagination... Well, I discovered I didn't really have very much - nor the inclination to work hard to cultivate it. Still, I had enough talent to find employment later as a freelance illustrator - and being freelance, I can choose to take jobs where I'm *always* told what to do.

Artistic? Like I said, depends how you'd want to measure it.

For the thirteen years he knew me he always called me 'Princess' - which is either ironic, given how much thought he put into choosing my name, or proof of how much of a romantic he was. During the first half of my time with him I remember everything being pink, as if - like 'Princess' - colour was another part of a template against which I was being moulded. When I realised I didn't actually like pink and told him so, well, he was devastated. "What colours do you like then?" Shell-shocked, the only way I could have made it worse for him was to say blue or red, boy's colours. So although I had no real favourites, I told him green and orange; they seemed 'safe' and relatively non-committal. As it happened, I actually liked red and was never really a fan of orange, yet over the years it is my love of green which has grown. Is there any other colour in the universe where you can simply walk outside and be struck dumb by the infinite variety of the shades on offer? Red or blue? Come on! And pink - *really*?

When he died none of that seemed to matter any more, though on my fourteenth birthday I bought myself a pink jumper as a kind of tribute to him. It was the last item of pink clothing I ever purchased. I still have it and wear it occasionally when I need to cheer myself up - not that it's the colour that works the oracle but rather the memories of him it invokes. And if I'm *really* low then I'll sit on the sofa enveloped in my jumper's pinkness and put *Dr No* or *From Russia With Love* on the DVD player and imagine that I'm seven again and leaning against him on his little settee in 'The Snug'.

Okay, so maybe a little of his romanticism has rubbed off on me - but don't tell anyone. Not that there's anyone to tell just at the moment. Thirty-four and my on-off love life is currently 'off', a status that is beginning to slide uncomfortably towards being the norm - though not for the want of trying. Of course there's no-one to blame for that other than me. I seem to have developed this pathological habit of sailing through the early stages of relationships right up until the point where *they* 'get serious', and then I flee. I don't think it's anything to do with love, but rather my twin afflictions of not having the imagination to see where things could go next, nor a romantic enough nature to believe in Happy Ever

After. The first of those - I would argue - you can do little about. A bit like my Art A-level, you've either got the imagination for it or you haven't. As for the second… Sadly, I think my dad weaned me off romance before he went. I'd been so saturated in it - smothered by his Princess pink - that knowingly or otherwise I've rebelled against anything too saccharine even since. Let's face it, nothing's forever, so why embark on a commitment predicated on a lie? Isn't that dishonest? Love's all well and good, but isn't honesty better? Though having said that, I doubt my dad would agree. Not that he was dishonest; far from it. But we all have a pecking order for those 'big things', don't we? Like Love, Honesty, Sincerity, Kindness, Authenticity - though don't ask me what that last one actually means! They're the major parts of ourselves we choose to endow with capital letters because we sense, instinctively, that they're important. I just happen to have Honesty in front of Love, that's all. Where some of the others go in the sequence I'm still trying to work out! My dad wanted to be all those things simultaneously; given they were all important, why did a person have to be more one thing than another? I guess that was one of the things being a Romantic - capital 'R'! - meant to him.

If you *are* biased towards one trait rather than another, it follows that one of those 'big things' must come last, that there's a personal attribute - defining who you are and how you behave - at which you suck, relatively speaking, even if you try not to. Perhaps it's all about investment. In my case - imagination aside (and I don't think it even warrants a capital letter, by the way) - I suspect some of the people I've been involved with would challenge my assertion that I'm honest, and might also argue that I'm far from authentic. Obviously that's not how I see it. They probably get so hung-up on how in love *they* are and *their* vision of the future, that when I put Honesty before Love, they can only see it as a kind of betrayal, as if I've been leading them on. I was once called a "deceitful, lying cow" as a result. Not my finest hour. But that just goes to show you, no matter how you see yourself, you're not in control of others' perceptions of you, the ones they overlay and choose to label you with. Princess? I don't think I was ever a Princess.

Occasionally what others think of you can be insightful. I've had more than one person tell me what I need to do is to take a break; not a holiday on a beach or a weekend in Paris, but a proper break. 'A vacation from yourself' one of them called it. The overall theory they seem to be espousing - as if I'd asked them for advice in the first place! - is that I'm stuck in a rut which is not stimulating. And more than that, I'm stuck there alone. They think I'm too glued to the past and not focussed enough on the future - yet, as I've already said, I struggle to imagine what might be around the corner. So when they say 'a break' what they mean is three months in America or Australia or somewhere like that, either working or travelling; probably a combination of both. A chance to see a different side of life and to get some 'perspective'. It's the kind of notion that would have appealed to my dad, not that he'd have accepted the challenge himself. A romantic notion such an adventure may have been, but he had his boundaries and those were very much geographic ones. When people have suggested I do something wild like that, I can get enthusiastic for a short time, but then reality pokes its head round the door and starts asking questions: what about work? what about the flat? what about money? Could I really go off somewhere on my own - even if I took my pink jumper with me? You get the idea.

Once, Grace, an old friend, made me sit down with her in front of her laptop and had me qualify continents 'in' or 'out'; then do the same with countries. She said she wanted me to focus, to try and see what the world might have to offer. We talked about climate and such like, and then she had me making binary decisions about coast or not-coast, winter or summer, English-speaking or not. In the end she triumphantly presented me with a shortlist as if her work was done and everything was settled: Seattle, the West Coast of

Australia, South Island in New Zealand, Hawaii. I still struggle to see all of the connections between those places, and wonder how she managed to filter the world down to just four options. If you'd forced my dad to choose between them he would have settled on New Zealand, no question. Why? Because it's the most like England. And if you forced *me*, right now?

I don't know. Maybe the same. Or Seattle. Does it matter?

I suspect the Ursula he'd had in mind - the one he'd hoped I would grow up to be - wouldn't have hesitated. She would have been straight down to Thomas Cook's and splashed the cash on some extravagant flight to Australasia via all sorts of places en route. Dubai? India? Vietnam? Singapore? Maybe even Japan or China. And then she would have dusted off that old suitcase - battered from the various trips she'd already taken (whale watching off the coast of Alaska had been her favourite thus far) - and started packing, hurriedly making a list of all the essentials she didn't have but which she needed for a four-month sojourn down under. Maybe that Ursula would still be there, the four months sliding into five then six; and along the way she'd have made new friends, started a relationship with a penniless artist or a wealthy sheep farmer, committed the rest of her life to trying to resist an Antipodean accent. Or she would have crashed from one adventure to the next, arriving home three weeks early, all her money gone, and having fallen in and out of love at least five times along the way. I wonder which of these versions of me would have made my dad the most proud?

I'd like to think it's the Ursula who did none of those things; the Ursula who stayed at home and lived her quiet, unexciting life; the one whose values were slightly different to his - and yes, the one who puts Honesty above Love, and doesn't believe in fairy tales.

After All This Time

Have you noticed how, on cold but crisp autumn mornings, if you stare at the low sun and scrunch-up your eyes you can make it look as if there's mist laying low over the land? Yet if it is a truly misty start to the day, no matter how wide you open your eyes, the mist never goes away. Why is that? Surely logic would suggest taking an opposite action should generate an opposite reaction. Isn't that Einstein? Or perhaps a case of 'some you lose, and some you lose'? I don't know. It just strikes me as odd, unbalanced, out of whack. But then lots of things do I suppose, if you take the time and trouble to think about them. Having said that - and have you noticed how, as soon as you say one thing, another immediately pops into your head, often to baldly contradict what you had previously thought, as if there is a part of you determined to undermine yourself, to always dispute and ridicule, to disprove what you say and think and believe so that you don't actually know what's right any more? Anyway, having said all that about taking the time and trouble etcetera, most people don't have any spare, do they? Time, I mean, not trouble. Certainly not enough sloshing around for them to be squinting up at the sky. They've got more important things to do, deadlines to meet, trains to catch, mouths to feed, bucks to earn, clothes to buy, drinks to drink, dogs to walk... And not doing things takes time as well because we have to think about those too, deciding *not* to do them, working out avoidance strategies or alternatives. "If it's not one thing it's another" as my old grandmother said. Or may have said. An approximation at least. Not that she has to worry about whether or not there is morning mist any more, nor the chasing of buses or boiling of potatoes. Unless there's an afterlife and it looks very much like this one. Which would seem a cruel twist, wouldn't it? I mean, "out of the frying pan and into the fire". That could have been another one of hers, couldn't it? If you had known her you would be able to make your own mind up; but as you didn't, you'll just have to take my word for it. But an afterlife like this one? And what would come after that? Where would it end? We could be worrying about some kind of heaven-or-hell scenario without realising that we were already living in perpetual purgatory. Some joke that would be. And I wonder what might be different, one world to the next, if anything. Like that thing about mist and eyes. Would there be a world where, when you *did* open your eyes wide, the mist would actually disappear? Or one where there was no Einstein, or the rules of the universe were altered in some way, or the number twenty-four bus always ran on time? You might want to argue at least one of those is too fanciful. But I *do* have the time, just at the minute. Well, for much longer than a minute, obviously. The opportunity to contemplate things because I have no cakes to bake nor trains to catch. I'd like to take the credit for being in such an enviable position, I really would. And I may do yet; you know, find a way to harvest kudos for my situation, my freedom. It seems only right and proper that I should; entirely logical in fact. Why should Benson take any of the credit? All he did was to fire me; *I* was the one who got into the position where I could be fired. Doesn't that make it all my own doing? Doesn't that make Benson something of a puppet of mine, playing the part I had assigned him, merely executing his role based on the situation in which I had placed him? One might even say 'lovingly crafted'. Not that I loved him, of course. Not in any incarnation of the word. He was a little man in all senses: stature, philosophy, fellow-feeling, intelligence, imagination. Had he been born many years earlier I'm sure he would have been a pen-pusher. Literally. And perhaps he *had* been in one of his previous purgatorial lives. It would have been fitting; a part he hadn't even needed to audition for. There are lots of people like that, aren't there? Those who seem to fit the niche they occupy, round peg etcetera. But surely that can't occur simply by luck. "Oh, here's a hole and I fit it perfectly!" Surely people have to whittle away - either at the hole or at themselves - to become even remotely comfortable. Which is something I have never found myself needing to do, hence, in spite of what I just said, there was still a little surprise in that final confrontation with Benson when he confessed he had to "let me go" - which, to be honest, sounded like a rather generous and most un-Benson-like thing to do. To be let go, to be freed. If you think about it, that's almost beatific, god-like. Which certainly isn't Benson, and therefore all the credit must be mine. Surely. But time - which is the ultimate gift of freedom, isn't it? - can be a tricky bugger. It's as if someone might turn round out of the blue and give you a lifetime's supply of your favourite sweets or cakes. I mean, I like a chocolate eclair as much as the next man, but if you had a never-ending supply of the bloody things, well... You'd go off them wouldn't you? They'd cease to be your secret little treat and become something else; mundane, normal. They'd go from special to not-special, just like that. And freedom and time is a little bit like that. Now I have a fridge full of time and I don't know what to do with it. Remember weekends that were magical, or that short holiday you took to Belgium or wherever? How much were they elevated from the mundane because you had to steal time in order to make them happen? 'Steal'. That's my word. You'd try and eke out as much as you could from every last hour or minute to make the most of things; you'd cram in one more museum or garden or ancient monument because you had too. Because time demanded it of you. "Fill me up!" it begged; "Use me, use me!" And you did, and it was great - maybe not at the time, but looking back later, utilising smaller pockets of time in remembering the larger ones. Sitting on the sofa drinking coffee after dinner: "Remember that weekend we had in Tuscany..." It's as if the experience has become doubly special: special at the time, and then special again in its recall. Like the payback on an investment - and one that keeps giving. But now, in my post-Benson world, there is no special time because I have it all. No looking forward to weekends because they mean I won't be working; Saturday and Sunday might just as well be relabelled Monday for all the difference they now make. Indeed, why not go the whole hog and call every day Monday or Wednesday (not that I ever liked the word 'Wednesday', you understand). Not one minute is 'outstanding' - at least in the sense of spending time, if I may be tantalisingly philosophical. Occasionally there are incidents which trespass on the memorable; there will always be those. But now they exist outside the framework that time - in terms of Monday to Friday, the weekend, the working week, holiday time, half-term, Christmas and so forth - used to overlay on those self-same moments. It's as if *what* I do has become detached from *when* I do it; the symbiotic relationship has been broken. Is that liberating? George thinks it is - though essentially because a) George is jealous, and b) George doesn't know what he's talking about. I've tried to explain it to him, this theory of mine. Perhaps the location of those conversations - the ex-Lounge Bar of 'The Frog and Parrot' - isn't conducive to serious discussion. There's always the background hum of other voices, and from the archway into the Public Bar, the sounds of music or shouts from darts' players when one of them manages to fluke a good shot. Once upon a time 'The Frog and Parrot' was *the* place to play darts; it had a reputation, won the local league three years on the spin. But then one of the star players moved away from the town and a second switched allegiance to another pub after an argument over a pint of Guinness. It was all downhill after that. When the new landlords Bruce and Shiela (sounds like an Aussie double-act!) arrived a couple or three years ago, they weren't keen on darts, wanted to promote a different atmosphere, talked about the place being "a gastro pub" - which it isn't, by the way. So the darts suffered, the team got relegated, then suddenly the matches stopped altogether. There are still a few die-hards who play friendlies of an evening - hence the shouting - but that's about it. George and I chance our arms very occasionally, the odd lunchtime maybe. If I was generous I'd say we were average at best - though all that really matters is that I beat him more than he beats me. Anyway, George struggled to understand my philosophy about time. He couldn't get beyond thinking me a "lucky bugger" because I didn't have to face up to Benson every day. "You can be as jealous as you like," I told him, "but it's not as much plain sailing as you think." He ignored that and often regaled me with what seemed a never-ending list of all the things he would do if he had all the time I did. Much of it revolved around his precious allotment and when he would plant potatoes and harvest carrots and such like. Most of the rest was typically George; just pie-in-the-sky ideas about going off to places he'd always wanted to see. In the first instance George wasn't the romantic traveller-type he imagined himself to be; and in the second, he simply didn't have the money. He may not have been on the same page as me in terms of freedom from the tyranny of time - if that's what it was - but when it came to lack of adequate funds we were like peas in a pod. Don't you think I'd be off galavanting about the place if I had a few more zeros on the end of my bank balance? Too right! Under those circumstances I daresay that I'd need to modify my philosophy about time somewhat - which, in and of itself, begs a different question doesn't it, the relationship between money and time? Actually between money and most things. Money can't buy you happiness? Well, I'd have a bloody good try! "Where would you go?" George asked me one day once he'd finished his own list and confessed to wanting to boogie with Balinese dancing girls and the like. Faced with such a question most people would either be like rabbits in headlights or come up with the few places they already knew and liked. My own approach was much more logical. First I ruled out the places I wouldn't want to touch, like Africa and the Middle East. And probably a fair chunk of the Far East too. There was also be a big lump of what used to lie behind the Iron Curtain that scored poorly when filtering for an engaging travelling itinerary. Then I focused on what was left - which may or may not have included South America, depending on the mood I was in. After that the key was not in immediately narrowing down the geography even further (that's a schoolboy error!) but rather to consider *how* I'd want to travel; there's no point going somewhere and then finding out how you have to get about the place makes you miserable. In my case I wouldn't want to drive. I hate driving. For a couple of years Benson had me on the road all the time; thousands of bloody miles, up and down, everywhere you went looking the same. It was an existence filled with motorways and service stations. I used to see those bloody blue motorway signs in my sleep. So no driving - *unless* I was being driven. In a nice coach; something small and exclusive. But better than that would be, in preferential order, a) trains, and b) boats. Always loved a train, and my soft spot for boats comes, I suppose, from the fact that my Old Man was in the Merchant Navy. Now he *did* go all over the place, including those countries you wouldn't see me dead in. Oh, when you're a kid stories about Kenya and Malaysia and such like are all very well and good - romantic even - but once you've grown up and have a sense of the world, it's like, *really*? Not that I'd be cruising in the kinds of rust buckets he used to sail in. Always fancied one of those elegant ships going up and down the Rhine or the Danube, or something more substantial for the Norwegian fjords or whale-watching off the coast of Alaska. See what I mean about needing to focus on how you'd want to travel? It helps define your choices. Not that I shared any of that with George, of course; I doubt he would have understood that logic either. So I just gave him what he expected to hear: named a few European capitals and that was it. I doubt he was really interested anyway. I mean, not *really* interested. Would my Old Man have been disappointed given his background? Seen a lack of ambition in my travel choices? At least I was making a choice, however theoretical; he just went where he was told, subservient to where the ship needed to be. He was a fitter of some kind - which probably meant a lackey with a big spanner. Used to talk to me about various bits of kit he'd worked on, but that was a very occasional interaction. Perhaps when he came home every two or three months he felt he had to try and fill my head with stories. He'd be around for a few weeks working like a regular nine-to-five guy in the dockyard, then all of a sudden he'd not be there, away again, and I'd not see him for ages. Often he'd miss the events that were important to me, like Christmas and my birthday He'd bring me back presents wherever he went but it was never the same. I guess he was doing his best to make it up to me, but every time he came home I'd have grown-up a little more, wasn't exactly the same kid he'd left behind. And he wasn't the same man either - although his getting older was of an entirely different order to my own. If at first his homecomings were awkward, they could only become more so. And then one day he didn't come home at all. Perhaps a couple of years prior to that I'd stopped asking my mum when he was due back; there didn't really seem any point. He'd turn up when he was good and ready - although she tended to give away a few clues in the days before he walked through the door: cleaned the house, bought herself a new dress. That last time he'd been gone about four months before I asked her where he was and when he was coming home. I'd expected her to say Singapore or Freetown or somewhere, but it turned out he was in Perth and was staying there - for good. He'd had a heart attack while ashore one day; bang, out of the blue. They'd rung mum and asked her what she wanted them to do with what was left of him and she'd told them he might just as well stay there, no point in him coming back in a state that was of no use to her. Not that was how she replayed it to me, but it was easy enough for me to piece the sequence of events together. Once she'd told me, I got the impression she was suddenly able to relax, as if she'd been holding onto a grenade she wasn't sure was *not* going to explode. And I suppose it was similar for me; no more strained conversations, unwanted presents - that kind of thing. Don't get me wrong, I did miss him in a strange way; his comings and goings had provided a routine of sorts around which we fitted our own lives, though in my case I had the advantage of school overlaying a much more robust framework. None of that mattered to anyone else, of course. I mean, when I went to work for Williams - Benson's predecessor many times removed - the company wasn't interested in your home life, what growing up had been like, what sort of kid you were; all they seemed to care about was that you had enough O-levels and could to knot a tie adequately. I guess I scrubbed up well enough. And it was a gentle introduction to the world of work helped by Williams being a bit soft - though I didn't realise that until he had been replaced. Perhaps his aim had been to get through to retirement with as little stress and fuss as possible, so he kept things simple and low-key. As long as the business was trundling along that was good enough for him. But such an approach wasn't acceptable to new owners who came in some time later; Williams was fired and Johnson-Brown arrived to shake things up. I was in my thirties by then. That was the beginning of a new cycle. After that, every five years or so, new owners would steam in with a fresh set of plans, fire the old management team, bring in their own people; we'd rebrand, refocus; there would be a new mission statement, new goals. I was good enough at what I did to avoid the fall-out - at least until Benson arrived on the scene. Caroline had been one of Johnson-Brown's recruits. She was tall, and as thin as a pencil; not skinny you understand, but she had no hips, and when you looked at her from behind she seemed to be entirely contained within two parallel lines. All of which was exaggerated by what she liked to wear: high heels; narrow, knee-length skirts; tight white blouses. Her breasts were of average size but being the only round things about her, against her general profile they were as prominent as if you'd taken Ben Nevis and dropped it in the middle of the Norfolk fens. Everyone was nice to her face, but behind her back they called her Barbie - after the doll - and speculated that she'd made herself the way she was in order to snare a bloke who'd be sufficiently blinded by her looks not to see her faults and thus take care of her for the rest of her life - at which point she'd ditch the heels and the skirts and let herself go to pot. They said she was working her way through the department. I confess I made my pitch too, though I'm not sure where I ended up in the pecking order. Not very high. She finished with me after our first weekend away - Cromer it was - her complaints and general demeanour worsening from the Saturday afternoon onwards. I assumed her malaise had been provoked by the squally rain blowing in off the North Sea. As I recall it now, on the Sunday morning she'd shagged me senseless first thing, then told me to go down to breakfast and that she'd see me there. It turned out to be a last hurrah. When she didn't show I went back up to the room to find she'd packed and gone. It was a departure which reminded me of my father. The next day at work it was as if nothing had changed; there she was all straight lines, clip-clopping along the corridors, smiling at most of the men, her hook baited once again. I never told anyone about my dalliance, though I suspect a few guessed. At the time I had no-one to confide in. Mum had died about four years earlier, leaving me the house to rattle around in. I didn't need three bedrooms of course, and was devoid of sufficient imagination to conceive how I could possibly use them - though if Caroline had worked out, who knows? Having said that, had mum still been around she would have seen through her straight away and I'd probably never made it to Cromer in the first place. Anyway, there I was alone in a house too big for me. Briefly I looked into moving to something smaller and more practical, but the mechanics of it appeared just too complicated and unnecessary. Expensive too. All those fees you had to pay, and for what? Yes, I could have sold the house, got something smaller, had change to spare - but what was the point? Post-Caroline, I actually contemplated telling Johnson-Brown what he could do with his job, fuelled by the notion of selling up and going off on some adventure - by train and boat obviously! I told myself I was still young enough - just about - and that, timing-wise, it was a perfect opportunity. Who knows where I might have ended up? It might have been good to walk those ideas through with someone - even George would have done, but he wasn't around then. It might have led to a different outcome. But inertia never really left me. It was too easy to stay in the house, the job; too easy not to think about things, not to take a chance. Oh, don't think I'm a coward. Would a coward have taken Caroline to Cromer, one eye on the 'happy ever after'? I don't think so. Actually, I like to think there was a kind of bravery in staying where I was, that I was achieving something unique; after all, how many people do you know who have lived in the same house for nearly fifty years, man and boy? Mum used to say "a place for everything, and everything in its place". I think she applied that to the both of us, as if the house was providing us our place, and that's where we were supposed to be. If so, then the notion rubbed off on me. The Old Man had no equivalent; the sea was fluid, always moving, and he with it. I think that's one of the reasons mum told the Service he could stay in Australia - he didn't have roots of his own, not really. They certainly weren't in our house, not in any important sense. And when I say I've lived in the house "man and boy", don't think I've kept to the same bedroom for all this time. I started out in the smallest - all the years I don't remember - then graduated to the middle bedroom, which was just fine. It had a window that looked out across our small garden with its dilapidated shed, and then down to the back gate and the ginnel beyond. I could see the heads of the dustmen when they came on Tuesdays, ferreting away, dragging those old metal bins by their twisted handles, adding a new dent in each one every week. Once mum had gone I decided I was due a change of scene and allowed myself to graduate to the largest bedroom. In my one gesture of domestic affluence, I paid three blokes to come in and redecorate the house. Nothing fancy, just a new coat of paint in most rooms, covering up the dated wallpaper. We agreed they would "freshen the place up" and use "neutral, muted colours". They walked me through some colour charts, and having settled on everything shades of off-white, I took myself to Scotland for a week and left them to it. Why Scotland? Well, I'd never been, and you could get there by train. I stayed in Edinburgh most of the time apart from an excursion to Perth where I spent one night. Although I did the things I was supposed to - the Royal Mile, the castle, Arthur's seat and so forth - I didn't really like it. By the Wednesday I was keen to get back home to find out what was happening to the house. But I saw out the week, and when I eventually got back I found they had transformed it. Walking through the front door was like one of those corny double-take moments where you think you've walked into the wrong place. It was bright, modern, clean; it looked like it had escaped from a magazine. The guys had done a super job, really. I'd been sceptical, but they'd known what they were up to. It was then - given that none of the rooms looked like they had previously - that I promoted myself to the front bedroom. Thinking about it now, maybe it was a bit like moving house - though without actually moving. The only problem was that the new walls made everything else look rubbish; old and dated, out of place. Someone walking in could have been forgiven for thinking that I'd picked up all the furniture on the cheap from a house clearance; that it had all belonged to some eccentric old man who'd just kicked the bucket. It was all so brown! Gradually I began to replace it. I started in the living room, then my bedroom. Money wasn't a problem given the house was all mine - no mortgage to worry about - and I had no expensive hobbies on which to waste my disposable income. After about eighteen months I'd redressed the whole place, most of the brown furniture had been banished, and the house looked vaguely modern. Maybe even Caroline would have approved, had she seen it. Mum, on the other hand... Well, it just wouldn't have been her thing at all. I still wonder if she would have regarded it as a betrayal. If repetitive worlds and permanent purgatory were to be true, perhaps she's somewhere else, presumably in a house looking a lot like our one used to, shaking her head and bemoaning what I've done to the place. They call what I did 'moving on', don't they? And I daresay whoever ends up living here after me will have their own views on decoration and so forth. Maybe they'll be closet Victorians and reinstate floral wallpaper and brown. I'd like to say "I hope not", but the fact is that I won't care. Why should I? One way or another I'll be somewhere else. Maybe I'll have found a new job; one so great that I'll have been happy to up sticks and move, lock stock and barrel. It's not that I can't imagine it, of course, it's just that I find it hard to apply it to me; what, for example, would that job look like? What would I be required to do? I know what I can do; it's what I've been doing for years. But lots of traditional admin has been taken away by computers and spotty kids. With that gone - and no desire to return to being a "road warrior"… Well. That was partly Benson's justification for letting me go, the fact that he could get machines to do half of what I did and more quickly and accurately too. It was a point of view I couldn't really argue with. When he coupled that with him recognising I wasn't having fun at work any more, and, in consequence, no longer very good at it, he said the outcome was inevitable. How could I dispute the first of those other reasons either given I hadn't enjoyed working for the firm for some time? But the second part? I still had my moments, occasional triumphs - though they were, I confess, increasingly few and far between. What I needed, I told him, was stimulation; but as it turned out, Benson wasn't in the stimulation game. When George isn't telling me how lucky I am, or fantasising about his foreign adventures, he will throw little prompts into our conversations about companies in town who are looking for staff. None of these 'opportunities' are anything like what I'm used to doing, nor would they pay as much, but George assures me they are "not to be sniffed at". The other day - after complimenting me on how I kept myself in shape - he pointed out that there was a warehouse on the business park just outside town who were looking for people. For a while I thought George was suggesting some kind of management role until I actually looked into it and discovered he was talking about 'Pick, Pack and Despatch Operatives' - or lackeys with scanners, rather than lackeys with spanners. However fanciful, that felt a little bit like endorsing my life going full circle, me imitating my father - though without the sea, the ships, the travel. Which was enough to rule it out, of course. "So what *are* you looking for?" George had asked when he came back from the Gents, almost as if he had gone there to give himself time to compose his next question. Strange as it may seem, it was an enquiry that struck me as especially valid. Oh, don't think I hadn't asked myself exactly the same thing, but when it comes from someone else, someone 'external', well, it endows the question will a little extra weight. Isn't that right? And therefore, it makes the answer a tad more important. There are things I don't need, obviously. I have the house - a semi-detached fifties' build in a cul-de-sac that used to look out onto open fields - and my car which, considering the number of miles it's done, I really should think about replacing. I'd managed to buy it cheap from the firm after Benson made it part of my leaving package, getting something else he didn't need off his hands. In addition to motor and mortar, I've no debts to speak of, no responsibilities elsewhere - though that's more by circumstance than design. It might have been nice not to be on my own, to have a wife and kids, to experience the growing up of children from a father's perspective. I do see kids grow up of course, mainly the neighbours', and am always amazed how fast things seem to happen; nappies to school uniforms to falling down drunk on the Market Square in next to no time. Caroline hadn't been my only tentative foray into the foothills of prospective fatherhood, just in case you were wondering. There have been - in Rose, Barbara and Cathy - other periods of brief passion and drama. Mum liked Rose, but Rose quickly came to not like us; with Barbara it was the other way round, Mum making sure she spiked that particular drink. After I'd had the house done up I thought I ought to see if I could find someone else who might like what I'd done to the place, someone who'd potentially be happy to live there, fill it with their own things. A divorcee with a six-year-old daughter, I'd met Cathy after responding to her 'lonely hearts' ad in the local paper. Having always wanted to be a nurse but finding herself thwarted by a bastard first husband who abandoned her when Gemma was born, she had made it as far as being a receptionist in a Doctors' surgery. Although not even a half-way house, she liked the work, was good with the patients. I had, I confess, high hopes. But Gemma never took to me for some reason, no matter how hard I tried; and when Cathy found herself having to make a choice between what she might have wanted with me and what her daughter wanted without me - well, there was no contest. She apologised and hoped I'd understand; it wasn't, she said, anything personal. When I told George, he just nodded and offered to buy another round. Based on the outcomes of those various not so near misses, I don't think I'm in the market for another try. Maybe I've become too used to my own company, not having to worry about anyone else; and if that's the case then George's question about what I'm looking for shifts to become "how do I want to fill my time?" Ruling nothing out, of course. Yesterday, for example, I drove the twelve miles or so to our local National Trust property. Considering the scale of their general portfolio it's a rather modest Georgian mansion, but the grounds are nice and the walled garden is splendid. I don't recall us ever going there as a family, and it was only after the Old Man died that mum and I ventured there for the first time. I was too young to be impressed by anything other than the choices offered by the café and the games they occasionally put out on one of the lawns. Mum pretended she knew the rules of croquet and then proceeded to let me win. It had been, I discovered later, a bastardised version of the game. We went once more before she died and then, as part of my reinvention, I decided to become a member of the Trust. It seemed to make sense; I thought doing so would encourage me to get out and about, and initially I had visions of regular weekend trips to places further and further afield. However, the reality is that I was put off by the prospect of too much driving, so didn't stray far. The upshot? I'm something of a regular at the Georgian place these days and try to go at least once a month to observe the walled garden as it changes across the seasons. They grow some splendid vegetables and have a restored hothouse which, Jack, the Head Gardener, assures me is one of the finest in the Trust's portfolio. He's biased of course, but it's difficult not to be impressed by its underlying wrought iron structure and the clever way the windows in the roof are opened by turning handles set at shoulder height in the back wall. Although he probably shouldn't have, one day Jack let me have a go at opening them. Having expected them to be really heavy, I was amazed how easily the handle turned and the widows edged open. It was a triumph of ingenuity, I told Jack; he said it was all in the maintenance. For some reason I have tended not to take any photographs in the greenhouse but have started to do so outside. My notion is to compile an album, a kind of log which shows how the walled garden changes across the seasons. It's only for me, of course, and I'm sure Jack and his colleagues have their own record, but they might be interested in what I eventually put together, you never know. On busy days - of which there are few - the place is filled with families and picnics, various children and dogs running about uncontrollably. The lawn games are inevitably popular and if you look out from some of the west-facing windows at the top of the house you can see the carnage unfolding below you; the shouts and screams of both children and parents are never far away. I wasn't a particularly shouty child myself. That's not me choosing to remember my childhood in that way but a statement based on the testimony of my mother. When I was well into my teens she told me that she had always been grateful for my placid nature, especially once my father had not come home. It could have been difficult, she confessed, what with her being a single mum and all. There were other mothers she knew - you could pick them out at the school gates, often by their smoking - who always looked tired and harassed; single women struggling under the burden of two or more unruly offspring. For the opposite of a paragon of virtue, she pointed to Jenny Westmacot as the archetype of what she herself could have been - and was so glad she wasn't: unmarried, three children by three different fathers, always missing something, like a good coat in winter or proper shoes. But given mum and Jenny were like chalk and cheese there was no way I could conceive of her letting herself go to such an extent. Mum always seemed to have certain moral standards she never let drop; they were one of the few things she insisted I adopt, and given I was a pliant child, never something with which she subsequently had an issue. "I'm glad I've only you to worry about," she said more than once, "glad we didn't have more." I never quite knew how to respond to being told it was a good thing I was an only child. On balance I decided I had the better of things compared to most of my friends at school, especially when I considered the competition some of them faced for attention or presents, or the pain of those bullied by their elder siblings. Yet there was a part of me that occasionally wished I had someone on-hand - a little younger, of course! - with whom I could have gone to the park to play football and such like. Fanciful or not, it was a mild longing that didn't hang around for any great period of time, and as soon as I started studying for my first exams I welcomed the solitude. I was probably fourteen or so when mum started to confess such personal things to me, as if I'd crossed a threshold which allowed her to talk to me more as a grown-up and let me in on what she was thinking. Not secrets per se, but that's how they felt at first, and it was a privilege to have them shared with me. I had often wanted to ask her why she hadn't sought to marry again after the Old Man died; I mean, she was still young enough and, although I suppose she was relatively plain, she had a lot going for her - not least the house. I can't remember whether there were ever any suitors, which I guess means there couldn't have been, at least none that were serious. I always liked Mr. Morris from the corner shop. Friendly, cheerful and generous, he seemed to be a good template for the kind of father a boy should aspire to have. He was also a United fan. During the summer when there was no football to go and watch, he played amateur cricket; once or twice I saw his photo in the local paper, smart in his whites, mid-pose, bat raised as he watched another cover drive laser towards the boundary. When did it become too late, either for her to have a new husband or me to be rewarded with a new father? Soon enough, I suspect. There was a narrow window of perhaps four or five years where it might have suited us both, but by the time I'd migrated to A-levels (in which I did rather poorly, by the way) I was already looking over the horizon at what might come next. It wasn't forward thinking or planning as such, but rather the preoccupation of an mildly enquiring mind. There had been conversations about the 'future', words wrapped in quotation marks, concepts discussed in somewhat hushed tones. From her perspective I suppose the future threatened abandonment - though this time of a more complete nature. If she had loved just two men in her time (and this had been speculation on my part back then), the first one had been deserting her on and off for years until his permanent sojourn in Australia, and now the second was surely concocting plans of a similar nature. Which wasn't entirely true. And as it turned out, I ended up going nowhere at all, taking the easy option of that job with Williams. "Are you sure?" she asked me, trying to disguise how pleased she was that I wouldn't be flying the nest anytime soon. "I'll stay until I really know what I want to do" I told her, convinced that working for Williams would prove to be no more than a holding pattern while I sculpted a far grander plan. Not that such a plan ever materialised - in the same way George's plans for exotic holidays never made it beyond the rim of a pint glass. I suppose I settled quickly, too quickly. Or perhaps I never became unsettled. Work was undemanding; I fell into it easily enough, found myself a niche. Having an income, being able to pay my way, fund the odd treat - a trip out for Sunday lunch perhaps - seduced me into believing that I was in control, biding my time; yet all the while I was being tied down, like Gulliver when he was on his travels. Except I wasn't going anywhere. And I wasn't in control. I'd given up my freedom for the comfort of a pay-packet and being looked after at home; kidded myself that I would wake up one day and know what I wanted to do with my life and that would be it, I'd be off on adventures. Does it ever happen like that? Before you know it the world has moved on but you haven't gone with it. I mistook change for progress. When Williams went and Johnson-Brown arrived I thought the differences he was making were taking us all with him; but they weren't, of course. They were taking *him* forward, and the business too; a few of my colleagues managed to tag along for the ride. But for the rest of us he represented no more than a slight change in the scenery. What do they say about moving the deckchairs on the 'Titanic'? Johnson-Brown, Caroline, the others that followed them; all markers on my journey, events that one way or another I misunderstood or misconstrued. Whatever 'life' was supposed to be, it was leaving me behind, gradually, surreptitiously. I see that now. Have seen it for a little while. And when you find yourself sitting in a pub with a loser like George speculating over Malta or Madagascar, sipping slightly flat beer - well, it's too late then isn't it? Life's gone flat too. I can hold my end up when it comes to discussing fanciful plans - moving away, a new job, exploring the world - but there comes a point when that's all it can ever be, talk. Because you need something else, don't you? A spark sufficient to make change happen. It takes no spark at all to let others' change affect you. "Try something new," Benson had said as I was about to leave his office. "Look on this as an opportunity for a fresh start." Fresh start? I'm not sure I would know one of those if I tripped over it in Sainsbury's, never mind being able to engineer one on my own. Still, I suppose something might happen one day. I might get a call from a recruitment company wanting to place me in a great business; or I might bump into a nice woman in the shops or at the walled garden, maybe on one of those autumn mornings just as the mist is clearing and it feels as if you can see forever.

Out of the Woods

He imagines his phone sitting on the familiar dresser, its white cable linking it to the socket from which it garners life. He wishes it wasn't there. If only he hadn't left it too late to charge it. If only he'd remembered to bring it with him. But isn't that the way of things, the taking for granted what is habitually there - in this case his mobile snuggled deep in his jacket pocket. Until it isn't of course…

Nearly halfway along his route when he remembered it, his right hand had patted the breast pocket of his coat as if that might disprove his forgetfulness. The compulsion to check was both instinctive and inevitable. For a moment he had wondered if finding it safe about his person wouldn't have been more disturbing, giving the lie to what he had recalled. Or thought he had forgotten.

One way or another there was a betrayal in the air.

There being no benefit in retracing his steps, he had pushed on, deciding after the merest pause to continue to the end of the lake and then, by traversing the skimpy footbridge across its narrowest point, make his way up the steep rustic steps which led to the wood. Then he would simply walk along the track for a half-mile or so and back to where he had parked the car. Twenty minutes at the most. Maybe twenty five. He had glanced at the sky trying to gauge how much light was left, as if hidden behind the clouds was a clock which might suddenly break cover and all for the purpose of telling him the time. Six? Maybe quarter to? He thought of his phone again. In less than a month, at exactly the same point in the day, it would be around seven p.m., evidence of the biannual hourly shift he had never really understood. For a few paces his desire for more light left him - a desire which was immediately resurrected after a slight misstep and consequent moment of imbalance served to refocus his attention.

When he had looked down at his boots, now almost black on account of the rain, it seemed as if the whole world had darkened. The green beneath his feet had lost its vibrancy, all gradations in both shade and hue - clues as to the subtle rise and fall of the earth - had disappeared, scuttled away as if to satisfy the imperatives of overnight hibernation. Though there were few down by the lake, the tree roots which occasionally stretched across the path had also lost their definition in the gloom, and he recognised that, once up the steps and into the trees, it would be like walking through a field of trip-wires.

He had never questioned whether or not he would make it that far.

On the fourth step he lost his footing. A slightly narrower tread and a patch of mud obscuring its unevenness conspired with the failing light and the uniform dark khaki of his surroundings to deceive him. Perhaps he might have maintained some degree of equilibrium if he had - at that precise moment - still been holding onto the rope handrail, if his left hand had not been freed to make its transition from one grip to the next. Like all falls, his descent had been both rapid and slow: rapid in that it happened quickly, yet also much less so thanks to the slow-motion overlay the brain can choose to apply to such disasters. The manner in which he had both stumbled and made a grab for the rail had been sufficient to start his body twisting and his foot squirming in the mud such that, as he fell, he turned a full one-hundred and eighty degrees before landing front-first on the ground at the base of the steps. Although he had managed to get his hands out in time to avoid landing on his face, his chest took much of the blow. Winded, he lay there for a moment unable to breathe, rapidly alternating between attempting to reorient himself and an almost theatrical gasping. A few seconds proved sufficient for him to fill and kick-start his lungs again, and to recognise where he had ended up; if he glanced up he could just make out the end of the bridge over the lake. He cursed himself for being a clumsy idiot, then tried to move.

The pain was instantaneous and of such all-encompassing ferocity that he found himself unable to locate it. "Shit!" he gasped. Attempting to turn so as to identify where he had been hurt, he found even the slightest movement only served to induce further agony. His breath shortened again. From his prone position he could see his hands immediately in front of him and in wriggling his fingers began a process of elimination. Both his forearms seemed mobile enough and when he tried to adjust the position of his arms as a whole he seemed able to do so. He pushed against the sodden earth and lifted his shoulders a little. He could sense the muscles tensing in his lower back, feel their sinews straining; that was something. But that was as far as he could go. As soon as he attempted to move his hips he was assaulted by pain once again, so eased himself back onto his front, lying prone. The damp of the trail - an irresistible combination of earth, rain and vegetation - was already soaked into the fabric of his jeans, consoling him that it was an intrusion he could actually feel on his legs. "Hips or lower then," he told himself aloud, as if making the diagnosis verbally would help to make concrete what was going on, the conundrum he was in. Such self-distancing had been a technique he had used before (admittedly at work) in order to better assess difficult situations, though he had experienced nothing akin to this. He had a logical mind, could work out strategies, make plans, knew how to get from 'A' to 'B' - and right now 'B' was his car, parked less than a mile away from the top of the steps. "All I need to do is make a call," he said.

And then he remembers his phone again. Or rather the absence of his phone.

Attempting to relegate the pain to the back of his mind, he tries to concentrate on process, identifying what he needs to do in order to extricate himself from his predicament. Knowing a phone call is an impossibility, for a few seconds he resorts to shouting, his cries for help seemingly absorbed by the trees as if they had wilfully become a barrier designed to prevent sound from escaping. He shouts and listens, shouts and listens. It is ironic that the woods seem to have turned against him, former benevolence twisted into a total lack of cooperation. Out of breath again he listens, hoping to hear the sound of footfall or the barking of a dog. It seems suddenly darker. With a shiver he tries not to tell himself that most dog walkers - indeed walkers of any persuasion - would be on their way home by now. He recalls an image of the car park as he had left it; how many cars had there been? Five? Six? And how many now? He suspects only one. Another shiver bumps the pain front and centre in his consciousness and he is suddenly compelled to cry out "Help!" once again, though this time in a voice he fails to recognise.

Focussing on his breathing, he establishes some brief semblance of calm. Remaining where he is not an option, so he faces a choice of either trying to get up the steps or returning the way he came: the difference of half a mile, the price being one steep incline against a gradual rise. Steeling himself, he tries again to lift his body from the ground - but the pain hits him as before. Crawling is his only option, and this in turn confirms he can only try and retrace his steps. It is a notion - retracing his steps - which suddenly makes him laugh, the joke being in the incongruous nature of the words themselves when applied to his predicament. 'Steps' is also, in both senses, somewhat cruel. "Breathe," he says aloud, then "this is going to hurt." And it does. Lifting his chest from the ground as high as he dares, he attempts to lever himself forward on his elbows. The pain is remorseless; his breath shortens again. He travels perhaps six inches. Another laugh, again unexpected, more desperate. "Focus!" he chides, then lifts himself again, drags himself forward a few more inches, perhaps eight or nine this time. The pain comes, then begins to recede - and he repeats the action. After a few minutes he finds a cycle of movement, pain and breathing that is almost bearable. Already his clothes are soaking wet. He has travelled perhaps three or four yards. As he pauses between efforts, he attempts to calculate how long it will take him to get back to the car - not because he needs to know, but because doing so will distract him from the pain. And then a voice comes to him from elsewhere in the woods, his own voice which says "this will be something to tell the grandchildren."

Had he not been concentrating so hard on maintaining his rhythm - move, pain, breathe - he would have laughed at that notion too, not merely because it was such an incongruous thought at that precise moment in time, but because of how Jassy had left him. This time there had been something about her departure which had spoken of finality, as if it were really the end. Thanks to a small multitude of such episodes - arguments over the inconsequential which then grew organically, became more personal, got to the nub of things between them - he had developed a scale for her dissatisfaction with him. At its heart was her wanting him to commit: marriage, kids, the whole nine yards; and ranged against that, unspoken by him yet surely all too plain from her perspective, his reluctance. Most times when she left him she went to stay with her mother or her sister; usually a day or two proving enough to reestablish equilibrium, for her to realise just how much she loved and needed him. She couched her return as a 'second chance' or a 'last chance', but thus far it hadn't really been either of those things. Her mother once confided in him that she'd always had a hot streak in her; she'd suggested instability. Jassy had tried to run away from home when she was thirteen, made it as far as the bus station. And at fifteen she managed to take the train a couple of stops towards London before her courage deserted her. So he waited, gave her time, knowing she was likely to be gone one, two, or three days, and that when she returned they would both be contrite, start again.

Move, pain, breathe.

But this time - just two days previously - her departure had felt unlike any that had preceded it, as if she were in an entirely different place mentally, applying not a pause but rather a full-stop to their relationship. Unusually, he found he had no idea how long she would be away. So this morning he had decided to go for a drive, and having driven, then go for a walk. He was familiar with the woods, the terrain; he knew how long it would take him to walk this circuit - long enough to clear his mind, and perhaps to find her waiting for him when he got home. Yet even as he parked his car, began his walk - and now as he crawled in agony away from the base of the steps - he knew he was kidding himself. "What grandchildren?" said a voice.

Move, pain, breathe.

He tilts his head a little as if doing so will help him differentiate sounds, hear better. Above all, he wants to be aware of any nuances he may have missed: was that rustle a bird foraging among the dead leaves or distant footfall? And was that a bark? Had he heard somewhere that squirrels made a kind of barking sound - or was it something else? He shouts again, throwing his voice into the descending gloom; but nothing is returned to reward him, not even an echo.

Another few feet and there, ahead of him, the narrow bridge over the lake. How far has he come? And how much further to go? Trying to compute answers to these almost irrelevant questions permits him to rest again, and he finds the excuse to do so suddenly welcome. He has already extended his cycle by inserting a shout into it - move, pain, breathe, shout, listen - hoping this will improve his chances, even if it slows his progress. Thinking about going home - and needing as much distraction from the agony as possible - he gives himself permission to sketch out future scenarios, all of which start with his rescue. He would be taken to hospital; they would operate; someone would retrieve his phone; he would make calls; be told to recuperate. What kind of future was that? The vagueness of it swirls about him like the sounds of the wood, sounds which he now struggles to identify, as if his radar has developed a terminal fault. He places himself in a bed, a plaster cast, the sheets white and crisp; he imagines the pain gone, and when he sits up he can look out of the window and see the town beyond - and further away still is the wood, this wood. And the bed becomes the mud on which he lies, the sheets are the leaves; his filthy clothes and pain are his only companions. Feeling something unusual on his face, he lifts his right hand and touches his cheek. A tear. He has been crying. Thrown by the notion - and shocked back to reality by a spear of pain - he chides himself again. "Focus!"

Move, pain, breathe. Move, pain, breathe.

Already he has given up on shouting. Driven on by his vision, he finds he desperately wants to be the man in that bed, no longer broken, no longer in agony; and so he tries to move a little further with each thrust, suffers the additional pain in doing so, takes less time to breathe. Although still crawling along, he feels as if he is sprinting now and arrives at the bridge more quickly than he thought possible. His efforts have blocked out all sounds other than those he has been making himself: the slurp of his body across the ground, the groan at each wave of pain, the heaviness of his breathing. But now there is another sound, that of the water in the lake lapping gently against the uprights of the bridge. The peacefulness of it surprises him and he finds himself propelled somewhere else once again; not to the hospital, but back home, sitting on the sofa in the lounge. And as he pauses at the entrance to the bridge, he finds himself listening into that future, wanting to know if he is alone or if Jassy is there rattling around in the kitchen, making a mess as she tries another radical culinary experiment.

There is no sound from that future of course, and he finds himself wondering whether that is because he is undecided as to whether he wants Jassy to be there or because he has no future at all.

To get onto the bridge he needs to make another significant effort, to lift himself over one small and usually insignificant stone step in order to be able to lay his chest on the wooden planks. It will be a minor triumph, proof of progress, something to give him hope. But as he does so, something around his waist - his belt, the top of his trousers, the keys in his pocket - catches the stone. Rewarded with pain the like of which he has never experienced, he screams and passes out, missing as he does so, the sound of walking boots thumping towards him from the other end of the bridge.

Through a Glass Darkly

Let me tell you about the town. From the window in the room at the top of the house you can see a ramshackle of roofs, vaguely haphazard grey tiles battling to establish the predominant direction in which to point. Framed by irregular windows and beyond the blackness of their glass, similarly uncoordinated lives move on, actors whose stages are often adorned with an ornament or vase on a cill looking out into the world, standing guard. And here and there, flitting in and out of view, phantoms of those lives, faces appearing for just a moment as their owners engage in dusting those self same trinkets or replacing dead flowers. Occasionally you might catch them in that vacant space between things - between thoughts even - perhaps looking down to the shops and pavements, the progress of others. Is that how I might appear at this moment should someone glance up from the street or from another window across the way?

Having to give myself a new name I settled on Paternoster, not because of its Latin meaning or religious overtones but simply because I liked the sound of it. Paternoster. It was a word which imbued something new in me; a gravitas perhaps, or a sense of worth; a word which was laden with potent, which said "there's something special about this guy, he isn't a 'Smith' or a 'Jones'". And even though I desired anonymity and a fresh start, inevitably 'Paternoster' disqualified that to a degree, the lure of it winning me over and trumping my ambition for invisibility. Lending itself to a type of elevator, a multi-barbed fishing line, a sea-side town in South Africa, an old hippie band, I was comfortable being added to its role of honour, choosing to refine it with the prefix of 'Ralph', a christian name I deemed appropriate for it, my age, and my target image. When the lettings' agent first repeated it back to me - "Ralph

Paternoster" - it seemed to fit like a favourite sweater. I handed over cash for the rent with a flourish, and he looked pleased.

But I digress. Immediately outside the house, the High Street comes to something of a shambolic conclusion. The succession of shops this side of the last remaining bank gradually declines in pomp until the whimpering crescendo of a charity shop and a second-hand bookstore. Our terrace then continues with three small cottages to terminate with this house, a floor higher and a room broader. Also not anonymous, I suppose. The other side of the road is less mirror and more cheap imitation. Perhaps it has always been thus everywhere in the world, the struggle for supremacy between north and south, east and west - or the tiles on roofs. "Always live north of a river" Saffie once said after an unhappy year spent shuttling back and forth from Vauxhall and Clapham. We had both been different people back then - and now here we were, almost within touching distance once again. Not visible from the house there is a river somewhere nearby, and I'm sure we must be north of it otherwise why would Saffie be here, living her new life in the road beyond the High Street, in that house with the blue sash frames, a white vase gracing the dormer window? New life but old name. Almost like me.

Which had made her easy enough to find; after all, no-one is invisible these days, personal profiles popping-up all over the place. We're all social media doyens now! Before I finally settled on it, I searched for myself - for 'Ralph Paternoster' that is - on Google, just to make sure I wouldn't be treading on any toes. Or vice versa. Importantly, as far as Google was concerned the new incarnation that was me didn't seem to exist, at least not in the UK. Isn't that where most people look these days to get their facts? "I Googled it" they say, as if the resulting information could only be twenty-four-carat truth. Search using my old name and you will find almost nothing but lies: rumour, innuendo and false reporting become substantive, like some kind of gruesome papier mâché mask; yet no matter how hard people tried to fix it to my face, the fit was never a good one. How could it be? I wasn't the person the mask depicted; it wasn't a true likeness. I was never the monster they made me out to be.

But that was three years ago. I wonder how quickly the time passed for Saffie; I wonder when she made the decision to leave London and move up here - and whether there were any intermediate stops on the way. Never having had the chance to say goodbye properly, the last time I saw her - across a room, not at a distance like now - she looked exhausted, worn through. If she had been crushed, that wasn't because of me; it was the process they put her through. You could argue it was all her own fault because she'd been responsible for setting the wheels in motion, but I don't think she realised how doing so would take so much out of her: the questioning, the cross-examination. We could have worked it out. I told them that. Had they left it to us then we would have found a way through and come to an understanding, an accommodation. But they weren't interested in nuance and subtlety; everything had to be black-and-white, provable or not, defendable or not. That was how they defined your character, by identifying which side of any particular line you stood. And by default they always seemed to take Saffie's position as the starting point, never mine: here she is, therefore this is where the line needs to be drawn. The question became where did I stand in relation to that line? Too often in the wrong place. At first I challenged them. How was any of what they were suggesting even possible given I was only motivated by love? On that basis, surely the only possibly place for me was on Saffie's side of the line. But they didn't see it that way. My defence lawyer, Hanson, tried to explain to me that they weren't drawing lines - to be crossed or otherwise - but building walls. "Why does she need a wall?" I asked.

He never gave me a satisfactory answer, though it proved easy enough for other outsiders to make up their own, drawing conclusions based on personal prejudices and perceptions. Everyone took sides. Most were nose-led by the popular press; it was an easy enough bandwagon to jump on. For some, their support for Saffie was based on no more than how we looked, as if that told them something incontrovertible. They refused to recognise that, having spent too long in custody, it was hard for me to look anything other than dishevelled. I had no access to the clothes in my flat and was forced to recycle the same things: wear them, get them washed, wear them again. Saffie was always well-dressed in professional outfits; sombre but smart. Hanson said that made her even more recognisable from the tv and the programmes people loved to see her in. They could associate with those; it gave them something to protect. Often she would be crying - which did nothing to help my cause. Harsh questioning and painful recall were the triggers, and the catalyst for much of that was when Hanson pushed her hard, especially if he sensed she was feeling vulnerable or on shaky ground. "Her memory of events that night is clearly not all it could be; she's hardly convincing. I suspect exploiting that lack of clarity may be our best chance." I wasn't happy with the approach, even if he was right. And I didn't like his word, 'exploiting'. That was the last thing I wanted. I told him that, and told anyone else who was prepared to listen - except few people were. The press continued to play on her celebrity and the fact that she was, to a certain extent, the new 'darling' of early evening TV; she was charming, open, accessible - and therefore vulnerable. It was difficult for her to have a private life; the affair with that slime-bag of a co-presenter - also plastered all over the place when they broke up - proved that. Hanson said that had been another opportunity for her to play the role of victim really well: "she's a professional, right enough". But that was never my perspective. Saffie needed looking after; she needed to know that there was someone who really loved her and who wanted to take care of her. Was that such a crime?

Perhaps my whole approach had been flawed. If I had to confess to anything then it could be only that - and surely such a simple mistake was not worthy of incarceration. Like I said, I'm hardly a monster. "At Her Majesty's pleasure" they say. Well not just hers as it turned out. There were people inside who liked Saffie just as much as those on the outside, so my cards were marked as soon as I walked beyond that razor-wired wall. Most left me alone, but those who didn't also refused to believe me when I told them I was innocent. "We're all innocent in here," one of the Lifers said to me. Some - the really warped ones - wanted to know why I hadn't gone further than just following her, or calling her, or sending her flowers. They wanted to know why I hadn't broken into her house and knocked her about, ripped her clothes off, tied her to the bed and… Well, you know. People in love don't do that kind of thing I told them. They laughed. "I used to love my ex-wife," one of them said, "and that didn't stop *me*". But I could never have done that kind of thing. Never. I told the jury that more than once - every time Hanson gave me the nod to do so - but no matter how often I said it, they didn't believe me about that either.

When they let me out there were some caveats; things I wasn't allowed to do - especially when it came to Saffie. So I kept a low profile for the first six months and used the time to find out what had happened to her. She'd left her tv role soon after the trial and then London itself a few months later. In her own way she'd gone to ground too. There was a bit of fuss at first - "Where's our Saffie?" one tabloid headline ran - but after a while they forgot all about her; she became old news, superseded by sex scandals, political controversy, threats of conflict over fishing rights, or the catastrophic shortage of Lego in the shops for Christmas. And because they had forgotten about her - and because I made myself almost invisible - they forgot about me too. All of which, once I'd found out where she had gone, gave me enough time to decide what I was going to do; to make a plan; to invent Ralph Paternoster.

She'd gone back to her roots, to small-scale journalism. The local paper made a splash when she asked if she could work for them for a while; I found the boastful two-page-spread digitally stored in the local library. "I want to remember why I went into journalism in the first place, and what I loved about it," she was quoted as saying. "Television is much less journalism these days, or about real people; often there's more celebrity than substance. I want to reconnect. Think of it as a research project." If she'd really meant what she said about television then she was in danger of biting the hand that fed her. But then again she'd been clever; that throwaway comment about research - perhaps a hook upon which she could hang a tv documentary about regional newspapers and local news-making at some point in the future? The vehicle for a triumphant return to the mainstream? If so, that was typical Saffie; subtle and understated. She'd never flaunted herself or her talent, and never used her good looks to get where she wanted to be. Not that I could see, anyway. You had to respect her for that. During the trial, a small number of insignificant people - evidently envious and jealous of her success - suggested she was naïve in all sorts of ways. "Look at that affair with Duncan," they'd say, "how could she not know what she was getting herself into?" The implication was that whatever happened to her - including me, presumably - was all down to her own stupid fault. But it tended only to be men who said such things; men who were firmly on slime-bag Duncan's side, and almost - but not quite - on mine. Presumably that would have been a step too far. When challenged, they said they'd been misquoted and that Saffie was an innocent victim, serially so; and that I was some kind of predator from whose clutches she had done well to escape. All of which proved they didn't understand - yet also hinted that they wished they'd been in Duncan's shoes, if not mine.

And I knew I *was* to be envied, no matter what had been said about me. How could anyone not covet the feeling I had for Saffie, the completeness of the emotion? It was all-consuming, total - I'd simply gone about expressing it in the wrong way. But now I was back; Ralph Paternoster would give me a second chance, ensure I didn't make the same mistakes again.

Ralph's plan was simple enough. Having taken a house in an elevated situation and from whose top bedroom window we could see across the town and through those blue-framed windows, he was going to keep watch, to establish Saffie's routine. This being horse racing country there was nothing unusual about him appearing one morning in the 'outdoor pursuits' store to avail himself of a decent pair of binoculars. "They'll help you spot the winners!" the man behind the counter had joked. Ralph had smiled and paid in cash. Quickly utilising his new purchase, he discovered the layout of Saffie's kitchen through one of her windows: the sink closest to the front of the building, shelves and part of the work-surface visible to the left. He could watch her as she washed up, and began to build up a picture of a morning routine which seemed to end with a short stint at the sink and then Saffie disappearing, the kitchen light going out. The adjacent window boasted frosted glass beyond which he saw merely shapes and shadows as she moved within. Clearly the bathroom. Ralph liked to imagine the detail of the person beyond, perhaps the semi-naked Saffie the glass masked. Based on how long the light was switched on and the time of day, the way her ghost moved behind the occluded pane, he thought he could tell whether she had showered or bathed, could see her vague outline when she combed her hair or brushed her teeth. I was only interested in routine, but Ralph seemed to want a little more than that. I didn't know that I approved.

Occasionally, even though I knew Saffie would be at work, I would still study her house, and then perhaps raise the binoculars a little to look out across the rooftops to the fields and hills beyond. On the white-railed gallops in the distance, racehorses were put through their paces twice a day, regular as clockwork. I remembered what the man in the shop had said and imagined myself an ace punter, scouting for the next Derby winner. I didn't know what I was looking for of course, and so all I could do was become absorbed in the rhythm of their movement for a short while, a vignette that helped pass a small slice of the time while Saffie was off somewhere busy being a journalist. It was during those periods I felt the most secure being out of the house myself, when I allowed Ralph to go about his business building up an image; when I tested him, fleshed him out, got to know him a little better. We had a routine of our own too; nothing dramatic or out of the ordinary, but enough to keep us occupied during the hours when Saffie was not in her flat.

I had decided Ralph should be artistic, and had acquired sufficient equipment to allow him to pass as such: a camera with a number of lenses housed in a proper camera bag; a small sketchbook and some pencils; a laptop. Often the locals would see Ralph taking photographs of the town, the stables, the horses on their way to and from the gallops; or sitting in the park drawing the trees and borders, or in the churchyard striving to capture the geometry of the Norman church. Of course no-one ever saw his sketches as Ralph made sure to close the book if anyone came near, and the photos were only ever downloaded to the computer. Personally I took neither seriously; Ralph possessed insufficient talent for anything he produced to be publicly displayed. And that wasn't the objective anyway. The laptop proved useful in fostering extended stays in the cafe we began to frequent. I had decided to undertake the challenge of recording my life, to produce an autobiography of sorts, though primarily this was simply a ruse to pass the time, which it did splendidly. Some afternoons I would check my watch to find - after three cups of coffee! - perhaps more than two hours had passed and that I was in danger of missing Saffie's return from work, at which point I would gather myself together, pay my bill - with the now customary tip for Mandy who always seemed to be the young lady serving me - and made my way back to my perch at the top of the house.

I started the autobiography with Saffie - it seemed the only appropriate place to begin - and doing so gave myself a framework against which to calibrate my present occupation. It allowed me to re-examine our first meetings, how I had come to feel about her, the events which had led to multiple unsavoury incidents involving the police and then the final legal denouement. As I charted and reviewed, I found myself able to sift and filter, to establish where in the past I had perhaps made mistakes. But the exercise also confirmed that of which I had been confident of all along, namely my feelings for Saffie. These - against the tribulations suffered, the trials endured, and the penance paid - merely demonstrated the righteousness of my present course; they validated the creation of Ralph Paternoster and the immutability of my plan.

Or so I had assumed. Two events shook me from the comfort offered by my hitherto unwavering certainty in my course of action. The first of these was a brief incident in the cafe. I had become so accustomed to my routine - typing at the table in the far corner Mandy had started reserving for me, engaged in the unwrapping of what Saffie meant to me - that I had started to ignore the 'ding' of the bell when someone entered, blanked out the comings and goings of the place. It was a reverie only ever interrupted by Mandy's arrival at my table to ask me if I needed any more coffee or to see if I could be tempted by the 'gateaux du jour'. One day - it was in the middle of my third week - I happened to glance up from my keyboard to see Saffie at the counter. I was immediately thrown into a panic. What was she doing there? It was still only mid-afternoon and she should have been at work. This disquiet was multiplied many times over with the sudden fear that she might look my way and recognise me. We *were* to meet, of course - my plan led up to that - but it was to be at a time, place and manner of my choosing; I hadn't allowed for happenstance to play a part. As soon as I had been able to take her in, to steal just a second or two to register her standing there just a few feet from me, I lowered my head and looked down at my computer. The letters on the keys swam before my eyes. And I waited, half-expecting her shadow to suddenly appear across my table, or - even worse - for a scream to rend the air. But for that to have happened she would have needed to recognise me, instantly and unequivocally. The intervening years, although they had clearly been kind to her (I could see that from my brief glance) had been harder on me. My hair had begun to turn quite grey during my period of incarceration and, as part of Ralph's profile, I had let it grow a little longer, subsequently choosing to embellish it with a beard of sorts. As I waited, my heart beating almost uncontrollably, I tried to persuade myself that Saffie would have needed to see me square on - my eyes, my nose, the shape of my mouth - in order to recognise me; and that, even if she glanced my way, all she would see would be an unfamiliar man sitting quietly at a laptop in the corner. When a shadow did fall across the table a few minutes later it was accompanied by Mandy's voice. "Are you alright?" she had asked, clearly concerned. I glanced up slowly enough to establish that Saffie was no longer at the counter and, as far as I could tell, no longer in the cafe at all. "You look a little peaky." I tried to smile, suggesting that I had just written something that had been both challenging and moving. She feigned a glance over the top of the computer screen. "Sounds interesting," she said, "and you've been working at it for quite a while, haven't you? Perhaps you might let me read it one day."

It was not the narrow escape with Saffie that led to the second disquieting event, but rather that final - and innocent - exchange with Mandy. I had not expected to find myself in a confrontation as a consequence of her comment, but once back at the flat it became clear that Ralph was beginning to have notions of his own. I had just about forgiven him for his trying to imagine a semi-clad Saffie behind her bathroom window (my initial view being that such juvenile desire was hardly threatening the execution of my overall plan), but it was evident that he now also had designs on Mandy which, if they had been brewing in the background, had erupted as a result of her demonstrating an interest in what I had been writing. Ralph seemed intent on taking full advantage. "Why not let her see it?" he had asked, deliberately omitting to overlay a veneer of innocence on the suggestion. "But not at the cafe, obviously. Perhaps back here one day, once she has finished work. We could make her coffee - just for a change! I don't think she'd hesitate, do you?" Although he'd asked, I don't think he had any interest at all in what I thought. He gave the distinct impression that he was hatching a secondary plan entirely independent from my own. "She clearly likes us; why else would she reserve our table or keep coming over to check that we didn't need anything more? You may not have noticed, but when we have cake we always get the largest available slice." It was easy to see through him; his motivation was nothing other than carnal. "Don't pretend to be surprised," he said, trying to sound vaguely affronted, "or try to manufacture some kind of faux shock. Your precious plan is all well and good, but what's the end game, eh? You make out that it's one thing when it reality it's something else entirely. Look me in the eye and tell me that you don't want to see beyond that frosted bathroom window as much as I do; that you're desperate for looking to turn to meeting, meeting to talking, and talking to touching. That's what you've always wanted, to get past first base. And you could have, if only you'd not been so lily-livered, tied up in your self-deluding romantic knots." I couldn't shut him up once he'd started. "Now Mandy might give you a chance for a dry run - not that it would be that dry, eh? Hopefully not! And she would give you a chance to validate what you really wanted, and whether it was right to keep Saffie up on that pedestal; after all, you don't want to upset her a second time, do you? Not unnecessarily, I mean. Mandy could be Saffie's insurance policy; did you think about that?"

Needless to say I hadn't. Although he was twisting things around to suit his own ends, I had to confess that he had a point; my recognition made him smile. The last thing I wanted was for Saffie to get hurt, and there was a possibility, however meticulous my planning or how careful and considerate I might try and be, that just seeing me could trigger an unwanted reaction. That's why my plan called for a softly-softly approach. "It doesn't matter," Ralph said, reading my mind. "It will make no difference how cautious you are. From her perspective at some point you will suddenly be there. You might as well leap out from behind a bush and shout 'Surprise'! She won't give you the chance to execute your precious plan; you won't have time to take it easy, one step at a time. You just won't. Once you make your move you'll need to be prepared to go straight to the endgame. All in. No hesitation. At all." He paused to allow his words to take effect. Then, in a more conciliatory tone, "So all I'm suggesting is that Mandy could give you the perfect opportunity to test out that endgame. If you find that it's not what you want and doing so demonstrates that the last step of your plan is flawed and is likely to give you no satisfaction whatsoever, then you can retire from the battlefield gracefully, quit this house, leave Saffie in peace and untroubled. That's all I'm saying. And you won't need me any more either."

As I stood at the window, binoculars trained on Saffie's darkened flat, Ralph's suggestion reverberated in my mind. There was some merit in it, not only in his suggestion that it offered 'insurance' for Saffie, but in that it did so for me too; using Mandy for a 'dry run' validated the plan and de-risked it somewhat. The thing I liked most about it was the discovery part, finding out what it was I really wanted. I had no desire to give Ralph any credit, but I had to admit that he was right about the 'romantic' in my intentions. That was how I'd always been, how I still intended to be; but the harsh reality was that romance requires two participants. "It takes two to tango," Ralph observed from somewhere out of sight. And what if they don't want to dance, I asked myself, effectively doing his job for him. I had myself down as a Viennese Waltz kind of guy, Saffie regaled in a gloriously white and voluminous chiffon number. But what if she wasn't? What if she was more a Rumba person - or even an Argentine Tango? Under those circumstances, a waltz simply wouldn't cut it; all that effort and planning, for what? I would almost be back at square one. Ralph certainly wasn't the waltzing type; he was more Latin than ballroom. Although I had not expected such an opportunity, did he offer me the chance to try out a 'plan B' without compromising the integrity of 'plan A'? "I bet that Mandy's a dancer," he suggested with a degree of certainty that was unnerving. What had he seen that I had missed?

Needless to say, my visit to the cafe the next day was burdened with a new tension. I had executed my usual morning routine with as much diligence as I could muster, including my vigil across the rooftops. As it turned out, Saffie was only visible - in either clear or ghostly forms - for a short period, and when the kitchen lights went out I checked my watch to confirm her departure somewhat earlier than usual. She must have been heading out somewhere. "The coast was clear" as Ralph might have said - although he seemed to be conspicuous by his absence.

Once I had completed my ablutions, I packed my little rucksack with my camera, the sketchbook, the binoculars and my laptop, and headed up out of the town to one of the hills that overlooked the gallops. I had decided to try sketching horses as they passed below me, aiming to see if I could get any sense of motion or power into my drawing. The camera and binoculars were back-up options in case my artistic endeavours failed - which they inevitably did - and so after about forty I minutes contented myself with capturing some long-range landscapes and following those potential Derby winners through my glasses. In the end it proved a relaxing enough couple of hours.

Perhaps I should have been on my guard when, walking through the door of the café after lunch, I found my usual table occupied. Mandy seemed to be at my side instantly, apologetic that she had been unable to hold it for me. She pointed to another nearby: "It's not the same, but hopefully okay…" The new location threw me, its vista inevitably different from that to which I had become accustomed. And even though I pulled out my computer to work - and even though Mandy managed to furnish me with an enormous slice of Lemon Meringue Pie and a free second coffee - I found I was unable to concentrate, my eye continually drawn away from the keyboard to the comings and goings of the staff and clientele. A little after two I decided to give up. "It's no good," I told Mandy when she came to check on me, "I'm afraid this just isn't working. I'll have to go back to the house and work there." "Is it far?" she asked. I felt Ralph - who had been quiet all morning - stir. "Just in the High Street; the three storey one at the end of the terrace, opposite the Cancer Research shop." "I know the one," she said, "I've always thought how nice it looked." What could I say to that? I gave her a brief run-down of the house, the rooms on each floor and so forth. "And where do you write?" she asked, nodding towards the laptop. "There's a room on the first floor, overlooking the road. I have a desk at the window. It's very peaceful." There was only the briefest of pauses, then, from nowhere, Ralph: "Why don't you come over and I'll show you round. You wanted to read some of my stuff anyway. I could make you coffee, just to say 'thank you' for you way you've looked after me these last few weeks." If I'd known he was planning to say anything like that I would have counselled against it. However, if he had surprised me with his sudden interjection, Mandy's response beat that hands down. "I finish at three," she said, "could I come over then?" We smiled.

Once back at the house I busied myself ensuring the place didn't look a mess - which it didn't, of course. If there's one thing I'll say about myself is that I'm a tidy soul. I made sure my laptop was fully charged and opened a couple of documents in readiness for Mandy's visit. Choosing which ones to show her had been difficult given I didn't want to expose anything inappropriate when it came to my history with Saffie; after all, I was now aware that Saffie went into the cafe too, and Mandy was sure to know who she was. I didn't want any alarm bells to ring, or for her to make connection between the me of now and the me of the past.

Apologetic, she arrived a few minutes late, still wearing her cafe uniform: a plain white blouse and a black skirt. Apparently Sue, who ran the cafe, needed to have a word with her about something before she left, and although she put on a brave face, it had clearly been a conversation which had unsettled her. Mandy declined to tell me what the subject had been, nor meet my gaze when she ducked my question. I tried to lighten the mood by proposing to show her round the house, an offer she immediately accepted. On the ground floor there was the lounge, the kitchen, and a small room inevitably called 'the snug'. Devoid of any distractions such as a TV or radio and merely containing a small sofa and a single armchair, it was where I occasionally read. There were two bedrooms on the first floor, and a third which was the one I used as a study. Mandy paused by the window, glancing down at the laptop. "I've got some things ready for you to read, if you still want to," I said. "One more floor first," she smiled. On the top floor there was a final bedroom and a small shower room, plus the room that looked out over the town. Going straight to the window of the latter, Mandy leant against its frame and pressed her nose to the glass. "What a view!" she said, "I've never seen the town from up high before." Seeing her silhouetted against the window, taking in her shape from shoulders to hips, I felt the pang of something both familiar and yet vaguely uncomfortable. Determined to chase it away, I offered her my binoculars which were sitting on the small side table where I always kept them. "Here, you take a look through these and I'll go down and put the kettle on, shall I? Come down when you're ready." She took the glasses and smiled, and I left her, back turned to me again, staring through the binoculars and out across the town.

I was halfway down to the kitchen when I heard a thump from the top room, as if something had been dropped. Pausing, I wondered if she had let the binoculars slip from her grasp; if so, there was a possibility that she would be following me downstairs soon enough, hopefully not sheepishly carrying damaged glasses. Then I heard another sound, as if furniture was being moved. Perhaps she had decided to sit down to look out of the window - but that made no sense at all as her view from a lower vantage point would have been severely compromised. And then I heard a scuffling sound and a muffled cry. "Mandy?" Perhaps she had called after me, wanting to understand something she had seen or the geography of the place. But then another sound - almost a shout - followed by more shuffling and something of a larger thump.

By this stage, thrown by the odd noises, I had become concerned enough to retrace my steps to the top floor with the intention of checking that Mandy was okay. When I got to the upper landing I found the door had been closed and, when I tried, I was unable to open it. There were still unusual sounds coming from inside the room and I realised Mandy might no longer be in there alone. Ralph! Leaning against the door once more, I tried to force it open. Perhaps he had wedged the chair against it. I called out, then started to bang on the door: bang, bang, bang. "Mandy, Open up! Open up, Mandy!" I became increasingly concerned, my frantic beating on the door transforming itself into a kind of hypnotic rhythm. "Open up! Open up!" And then suddenly, as if unlocked by the crescendo to which my pleading had risen, the door gave way and I fell into the room. Immediately in front of me was a chair knocked onto its side, and between it and the far wall Mandy lay on the ground. "Ralph!" I shouted, expecting to find him there; but when I looked around, he wasn't in the room. Mandy's blouse had been torn and her right breast had been released from the confines of her bra; her skirt had been lifted and was rucked-up around her waist; her knickers had been removed and her pale legs, slightly apart, were fully exposed. I could see a neatly trimmed tuft of dark pubic hair, and at the top of her left hip near her pelvis, the tattoo of a small red heart. There appeared to be a small damp patch on the carpet between her legs. She wasn't moving. I didn't even know if she was breathing. She looked like someone who had been frozen while making angels in the snow.

Momentarily stunned, I then cast around the room as if looking for something else that was supposed to be there - or to verify that something wasn't - and my eyes quickly settled on the binoculars which now lay on the floor at the foot of the window. Unable to understand what had happened or where Ralph had disappeared to, I walked over and lifted them to my eyes, instinctively training them on the flat with the blue window frames. Doing so I saw movement behind the frosted bathroom window; it was a figure I wasn't sure I recognised. Perhaps a shape that shouldn't have been there. Was it possible Ralph had made this way there already?

"Saffie!" escaped as a strangled shout from my mouth. Dropping the glasses to the floor and tucking in my shirt, I ran out of the room and rushed down the stairs and into the street, my only objective to prevent another catastrophe, this time in the flat with the blue windows.

Extra-curricular

There had always been three of them; the trio of boys who came top of the class in every subject, in one order or another, like a perpetual academic dance. Their monopoly smacked of an unspoken arrangement; a secret cartel which wielded power and influence not only over their fellow pupils but over the teachers too, teachers who wanted to devise ways of giving the rest a chance, a shot at glory. Yet if they made the weekly tests easier, the triumvirate scored a hundred percent; made harder, and the gulf between them and the also-rans was only exaggerated.

At first innocent of their superiority, once they came to realise how gifted they were it was easy enough to build a moat around themselves. They created a kind of democratic Camelot peopled by just three knights, each one taking turns to be king; and although they had no need to do so, they were happy to perpetuate myth and legend - like that week when they collectively chose to ace every challenge presented in order to make it impossible for the staff to separate them. The same had been true at the end of their first academic year, forcing the headmaster to award them joint first prize for their cohort's annual achievement award. In consequence, second and third places were cancelled; there were no runners-up. Only when they narrowed their fields of study for GCSEs did anyone else get a look-in, though never for first place. It was a dominance exercised every year up to their first year as A-level students. New pupils would arrive from time-to-time and, for the briefest of moments, perhaps threaten to shine as brightly; yet in the end all were eclipsed.

Given their uniformity of academic excellence, it was perhaps a surprise that their backgrounds, upbringing, and domestic situations should be so different - and all the more remarkable that outside of the classroom their tastes and appetites varied wildly.

Spencer excelled as the athletic one, physically beyond the margins of the average; he was slightly taller, slightly stockier, stronger yet more nimble, explosive, persistent, determined. He moved with an elegance and easy grace most evident when he had a football at his feet or a tennis racquet in his hand; yet his approach to such supremacy never traversed the borders of arrogance. Top scorer in the junior football team, he became captain of the seniors two years earlier than he should have. Inevitably an all-rounder, he threatened to make county under-16s for cricket, and was the school badminton champion four years in a row. However, in spite of his physical superiority, he approach sport with the kind of diffidence displayed in relation to his studies: it was all too easy, so significant effort seldom required; only when his dominance was threatened - like the year he was taken to a deciding set in the tennis competition - did he show anything like a mean streak. When people talked of sporting scholarships at university or future England call-ups (if only he could decide in which sport to major!) he would brush the notions aside as if irrelevant. For the other two, Spencer was either at the pinnacle or the base of their triumvirate, depending on the prevailing situation.

In spite of Spencer's considerable prowess, on occasion he was socially gauche and insecure, at least until he was fifteen or so. For many - especially his teachers - there was something incongruous about a boy with so many advantages, displaying discomfort in public situations as often as he did. Such reserve was not an ailment from which Alistair suffered, however; completely the opposite in fact. Although less physically adept than Spencer - yet no more nor less intelligent - Alistair's extrovert confidence was born of privilege, knowing he could get his hands on whatever he wanted. The only son of a father who was a successful City trader and with a renowned historian for a mother, his early childhood had been cushioned in the extreme. Where Spencer's dominance was manifest on the sports' field, Alistair's arrogance was born from something less visible but equally tangible: wealth. If his companion was first among equals when it came to physical endeavour, Alistair was always the first to possess the latest technological gadget, the first to have travelled to far-flung places. And given his greatest weapons were charm and self-confidence, he proved articulate enough to be able to extricate himself out of - and into - almost any situation; teachers loved him because he could be relied upon to shine publicly. It was his natural milieu.

And then there was Russell. On the face of it Russell offered the world nothing other than his academic prowess: there was no extra-curricular activity over which he could demonstrate superiority, no area of personality or endeavour in which he shone brighter than anyone else. He was physically mediocre and average at games, and his background was so diametrically opposed to Alistair's that on the whole he seemed an odd adjunct to the other two. If you were being generous you might have described his upbringing as 'modest' - even if 'challenging' and 'deprived' may have been far more appropriate adjectives. In the care of parents who didn't understand him, as a young child he had worked hard and independently to build up his stock of knowledge, to decipher how the working world functioned, and to hone his skills when it came to taking tests or articulating answers to questions, theories, propositions. None of it had come easily to him. Yet it would be a mistake to think that hard-won intelligence, sharpened to be the best it could possibly be, was Russell's only notable attribute. Buried beneath his unremarkable outward persona lurked an extreme romantic, a boy who cultivated a passion for - and unswerving faith in - the supremacy of the emotional life. Romantic with a capital 'R'. Where Spencer and Alistair's non-academic excellences were always in plain sight thanks to the way they competed or behaved, Russell's passion was hidden at a depth impenetrable to everyone except himself.

Given the three of them were clearly not peas from the same pod, one might be forgiven for regarding their alliance as a little surprising; it was as if they had agreed on a truce without ever going to war. Had you asked them, both Spencer and Alistair might have suggested that fighting to be academic 'top dog' would have been such a waste of energy - energy better spent elsewhere - that there had been no point going into battle in the first place. Disingenuously or not, Russell would probably have countered that, in his case, keeping up with his two friends was sufficient struggle in itself - and a constant one at that. Few would have disbelieved him.

As they progressed through their GCSE years, their academic brand became so strong that, in the sanctity of the staff room, teachers would often refer to them as a collective even when using just one of their names; if Ms Taylor remarked that Alistair had excelled in her last maths test, her colleagues would inevitably assume that the same was being said of Spencer and Russell. Once, Mr Parkinson - himself a somewhat romantic soul - had likened them to the Three Musketeers, but had been immediately shot down by his peers on the grounds that in a straight physical fight only one of them - Spencer - could possibly emerge victorious. For any member of staff who had been there at the time and then recalled the exchange a while later it would, in hindsight, have seemed potentially prophetic.

Although A-levels saw them diverge somewhat - Economics, Sports' Management and Geography for Spencer; Physics, Mathematics and Sociology for Alistair; and English, Philosophy and History for Russell - initially they managed to maintain their comradeship as if it were a magnetism impossible to deny. The first week or two they could still be seen eating together at lunch. 'Comparing notes' was how some of their detractors had come to view such liaisons, jealous of the triumvirate as if they were keeping tabs on the rest of their cohort and ensuring that what one knew, all three knew. Were that indeed the case (and to a certain extent it was!) then it could be argued that their reach and influence grew even more once they had been academically separated; and if opportunities for competition and direct comparison had been removed (Ms Taylor now only taught Alistair, for example) they still managed to give the impression that their desire to monopolise the academic podium remained undiminished.

However, trouble - which they had pretty much managed to avoid throughout their previous five years together - arrived early during their first year-twelve term. Two nearby schools had recently closed their own sixth-forms and as a result the respective A-level students were, by default, enrolled in the only local option, the boys' own well-respected educational establishment. Given a number of the less academically able sixteen-year-olds had left there after GCSEs to go to technical college, the new intake did little to alter the size of classes - though it did introduce outsiders who might conceivably have been as gifted as the triumvirate. Yet the threat, when it materialised, had nothing to do with the academic.

Susanna was never going to be any kind of intellectual superstar; her GCSE grades had been unspectacular and she arrived unheralded. There were a few newbies who came with something of a reputation - like the ex-captain of Somerstown's cup-winning cricket team, or the second son of a popular but minor television celebrity - and it had been on these Spencer and Alistair had initially focussed. From Russell's perspective, by default all new students were of little interest to him. Having said that, it was with Russell Susanna first registered - not as a result of her knowledge of literature, history or philosophy, but because she appeared strikingly familiar to the Ophelia depicted in Millais' famous painting. And as if that were not enough, the fact that his class was studying Hamlet in the first term struck him as more than mere coincidence. With the enigmatic and somehow mysterious Pre-Raphaelite Susanna sitting just across from him for several hours a week, Russell felt the hand of Fate on his shoulder. Fate. In his case it was another word requiring a capital letter.

Thanks to her also studying Geography and Sociology, Susanna was exposed to both Spencer and Alistair in equal measure, and while they were unable to make any artistic or Shakespearean link, they soon discovered she had attributes to which they could easily relate. Susanna was slim and reasonably athletic, and made a decent enough fist of netball for Spencer not to miss the fact that she'd made the sixth-form squad. And thanks to a passable singing voice and a willingness to throw herself into the drama society, she was soon endorsed with a minor degree of celebrity which Alistair couldn't possibly fail to notice. It was, therefore, the individual strands of her personality - in addition to her good looks - which drew the boys in. Not only did she possess a somewhat heady mix of talents, she did so against the landscape of their burgeoning manhood; it was like sewing a seed in especially fertile ground.

Not surprisingly perhaps, sex was a field Spencer had already attempted to plough. He had done so inexpertly at first, though his beginning to get the hang of things had been the reward for preliminary experimentation with various potential partners. He knew he was likely to be regarded as what might be described 'a catch', and had played his hand accordingly during the latter half of year eleven primarily thanks to encounters at a couple of Christmas parties which - although clumsy and not totally 'conclusive' - had set him on his way. At Amanda's birthday party in mid-February he had finally enjoyed his first satisfactory outcome (at least from his perspective), an experience upon which he judiciously built during the six months prior to sixth form. If he was conscious that in doing so he was also beginning to build something of a reputation for himself, he never said; and if it was something about which Alistair was aware, he didn't let on.

In any event, Alistair was merely a step or two behind. By this point he'd had - in theory at least - a long-term girlfriend for some while. Casey was the daughter of a friend of his father; he had known her for years, and though she lived sufficiently distant from him to be a pupil at a school on the other side of the county, they had met regularly enough for a bond to have been formed. Alistair's experiments with Casey had been both shared and democratic, explorations that were marked by mutuality, consideration and caution. The summer holidays had offered them their watershed; yet in arriving at such a defining moment, Alistair found himself psychologically released from Casey - this in complete opposition to the strengthening of her attachment to him. Thus, although he was content enough to keep up the pretence, he arrived into year twelve with an entirely different mindset and 'on the hunt' for the first time in his life.

Unsurprisingly Russell had yet to move beyond fantasy and the regular relief offered in the privacy of the shower. It wasn't that his desires were weaker than those experienced by Spencer and Alistair (if anything they were stronger!), rather he was held back by an inability to execute, lacking the instinct to know how he should go about losing his virginity. Deprived of the confidence bestowed by sporting prowess or natural extroversion, Russell had nothing upon which to fall back. He was resigned to suffer in silence, believing that one day lightning would strike, all the relevant pieces would fall into place, and nirvana would present itself. Fate again. Wasn't that what happened in novels? When Susanna arrived, Russell couldn't help but feel - or even *know* - that she was to be his lightning.

For her part, even though Russell's infatuation with her was obvious and not unflattering, it failed to ignite any spark. It was the same with Spencer and Alistair who, in their individual ways, were much more up-front in expressing an interest in her. Initially Susanna found it amusing above all else, and she assigned their various attentions to being the natural byproduct of having new female students on the roster. If she looked hard enough she thought she could see other girls who were similarly on the boys' radar (well for two of them perhaps) and so dismissed their interest as temporary and more or less innocent. She hadn't been so sure about Russell, however. 'Still waters run deep' she told herself, and in his case the water seemed very still indeed. What Susanna had failed to appreciate - and how could she, given she was new to the environment? - was the secondary impact her presence would have on the relationship between the boys themselves.

Alistair had mentioned her first. The three of them had been at lunch and - coincident with a lull in the conversation - he happened to catch sight of her across the hall. His remark had been reasonably innocuous, but not so uninterpretable for Spencer to burst out laughing and challenge "Not if I get her first!" All light-hearted bonhomie, it had been over in a minute and their conversation moved on to Spencer's recent hat-trick. Alistair had countered with news that his father was going to be on a day-time TV show the following week. In both exchanges Russell had said nothing, and to any long-term observer of the boys, such had been the pattern for the previous five years: boast and counter-boast, none of it particularly serious. Their mutual understanding always held sway; they maintained an unspoken respect for each other; there was no oneupmanship. This was how balance had been maintained. Yet would that same long-term observer have noted the slight edge in Spencer's tone, the way he started to watch Alistair when he wasn't looking? Would they have seen the secondary glance Alistair offered the hall in order to relocate Susanna? And would they have seen Russell colour slightly, the skin around his jaw become marginally more taught? Surely there was nothing in him giving additional focus to his cutlery; he was just Russell after all.

But soon everyone did notice. Susanna was the first. She started to find both Spencer and Alistair in locations that were vaguely foreign to them. They began to be more attentive in the classes they shared, keen to help - or to seek help; the distances they maintained from her reduced, and in Spencer's case - who had already come close to crossing some kind of line - that meant the occasional brushing of an arm, a shoulder. What had begun as amusing was beginning to shift into being something else. And Russell? Russell was the opposite: broodier, quieter, more withdrawn - and when she needed to talk to him in the context of an assignment or because she thought he could help her with something, he was even more monosyllabic than usual.

The staff saw different things, of course. On the playing fields they saw Spencer fiercer in the tackle, faster in the sprints; he seemed to have inherited a new kind of energy that required burning off, new goals that needed to be broken, new records set. Alistair was more voluble and sociable than ever, volunteering to be involved in events - even Drama! - which had until that point remained outside of his normal purlieu. They assumed he was working his way up for a tilt at Head Boy in year thirteen, and so they encouraged him. They encouraged them both. And Russell? In Russell they saw little change, apart perhaps for an increased drive for better marks, higher grades.

Then everyone began to notice that something was amiss. Even though they shared no lessons, more than ever the classroom became a virtual battleground as they worked to enhance their supremacy - especially in Geography and Sociology. In the staffroom, Ms Taylor expressed concern that Alistair was trying too hard and beginning to show signs of fraying at the edges. It had been the signal to permit discussions on all three of them, of course. Only Mr Thomas lauded Spencer's new-found drive as it had helped propel the football team into the quarter finals of the inter-school cup. No-one expressed any particular opinion about Russell, other than to say his work was showing signs of greater depth and maturity. Mrs Francis' mention of Oxbridge was met with knowing nods.

When their ritual coming together at lunchtime was abandoned one Tuesday with Alistair crying-off because of something to do with Drama, and then, two days later, with Spencer preferring an additional training session in the gym (where the netball girls happened to be working out too), the notion that something fundamental had broken came upon their observers pretty much simultaneously. Increasingly Russell could be seen sitting alone while Spencer and Alistair pursued something extra-curricular - often not entirely unrelated to Susanna.

For her, what had begun as mildly amusing was now sliding dangerously toward being something else. Her friends started making comments about Spencer and Alistair, telling her how lucky she was, how envious they were, how she would have to choose and put one of them out of their misery. Trying to laugh it off only worked for a short while. No-one mentioned Russell, yet Susanna knew he was implicated because he was their friend - and because he was behaving in an increasingly odd way, even for him. She wanted to talk to someone, to express her concern, her discomfort. The obvious route would have been to speak to a member of staff, but her desire to shy away from anything so formal left her limited options.

In the week before half-term two events brought matters to a head. Although no-one was able to identify the catalyst, the first of these was a very public argument between Spencer and Alistair outside the sixth-form block at the end of Wednesday's lessons. The dozen or so people who witnessed it were initially drawn to the confrontation on hearing raised voices; from their tone they could tell it was not simply banter. They saw Alistair poke Spencer in the chest, not once but twice; they heard Spencer tell him to stop; they saw Alistair press harder. The punch Spencer threw came from nowhere - like lightning - and although not connecting as cleanly as perhaps intended, was sufficient to send Alistair to the ground. The following day the school was buzzing with the news; witnesses were sought, those who had actually been there became celebrities of a kind. Reports of what happened began to vary driven by that celebrity and the desire to be instrumental in the creation of a new legend. Neither boy was in school. Some members of staff interviewed Russell assuming that he would know what happened. He said he had heard the same reports as they; that was all he could offer - even though he knew the cause of the disagreement.

Then, on the Friday morning, Susanna sought him out first thing. She was confused, in tears; she wanted to know what was going on, and how she could stop it. Or how he could stop it. "Stop what?" he had asked. Spencer had been waiting for her in the park across from school at the end of Thursday. He had made his play in a rough, brutish way. He had sworn hatred for Alistair. Susanna said that before he was frightened off by the presence of others, he had 'touched her'. At that precise moment, after relaying her story, she was only too willing to accept the hug Russell offered; even something vaguely comforting went some way to assure her that she would be okay. When he released her, he told her to speak to the Head. There was, he said, little they could do themselves - although the one other thing he *did* do was to go and see Alistair at the end of the day. As a triumvirate they may have ceased to be friends, but there remained some lines which should never be crossed.

When school reconvened after the half-term break it did so without Spencer, Alistair and Russell. And Susanna. She had been excused on medical grounds, the stress that had been building over the final few days of the previous half-term taken to a new level as a result of what happened over the holiday. Alistair and Russell had been temporarily suspended from school until various investigations had concluded, the majority of which were entirely outside of the academy's control. Spencer would never be going back.

Two dog-walkers had found his body in the midst of a clutch of rhododendrons in the park. It had not taken the pathologist long to establish that he had been hit on the head from behind before being stabbed. A knife had been found in the grass nearby; there were no fingerprints, no witnesses. The blow to Spencer's head had been sufficient to disorientate and immobilise him; the knife had dealt the fatal blow. Such a conclusion was, the pathologist said, beyond doubt; whether the same hand had been responsible for both actions he couldn't say. The investigating officer didn't think it really mattered whether it had been one, two or three people; murder was murder, after all. And the knife? The kind used in mass catering - especially in school canteens.

Steak

"My dad taught me how to cook steak. Minute-and-a-half, turn over; minute-and-a-half, turn over. Made out like it was a big deal; one of the secrets of the universe. So when I left home and had to fend for myself, I tried it. Worked like a dream, though not at first. I did the 90-second turn over thing four times like he showed me, but it was still too bloody in the middle. Then gradually - after quickly going up to six turns then eight - I found a pattern that worked. Ten flips. You may say that's quite a lot, but I like my steak well cooked - I don't mean cremated, but with hardly any pink in the middle.

"And he was half-right about it being a useful skill to have - cooking steak I mean. I'd been good friends with Alice since we'd met at college; nothing special, you understand, just friends. Then we went our separate ways but kept in touch. About eighteen months later, as coincidence would have it, she moved into town. I don't think she knew very many people here at that stage, so she invited me over; she wanted to show me her flat, talk about old times, not feel lonely. I offered to cook her steak - which proved to be so nearly a disaster but then turned into something else.

"You see I'd only ever prepared steak on my own cooker and didn't realise that how long you cooked it for depended on the hob as much as anything else. Electric versus gas. You know, that sort of thing. Anyway, on Alice's gas hob I started out flipping the sirloin as usual but after only a few turns the outside of the meat was already charring; if I'd kept going for the full ten turns I would have had nothing left. So I took it off the heat, let it rest, then served it up - all the while hoping it was actually done inside.

"And it was. A little pink for my taste, but Alice thought it was fantastic. Best steak she'd ever tasted, she said. Maybe she looked at me a little differently after that. Or maybe it was the wine. Twenty minutes later I found myself in her bed - and Alice turned teacher.

"Not that I'd ever had any trouble in that department, you understand, but Alice was clearly - what shall I say? - more experienced than me. Anyway, we seemed to hit it off (if I can use that phrase) and for a while we were an item. How long? Not very; a few weeks I suppose. Then, what with her job and all, she started to meet new people, her social life began to expand. There was no big denouement, we didn't have a row or anything; I guess I just faded out of the picture. She probably found someone else to cook her steaks for her."

~

"I suppose I always had a soft spot for Pip - though he didn't like me calling him that! In the early days he used to protest that his name was 'Phillip', but I didn't care. Then he said he'd make an exception in my case - not that he could have stopped me anyway. I think he reminded me of the character from *Great Expectations*, though I never told him as much. Doubt he would have got the reference.

"It was ironic that I moved to where he lived. Do I mean ironic? Lucky? Fate? Unfortunate? But it helped in the early days when I was new there and didn't know anyone. We used to meet up quite often. And then once day he suggested he come round and cook me dinner. 'A kind of treat' was how he put it. I confess when he made the suggestion I immediately had a different kind of 'treat' in mind. After all, it had been several months since I'd split up with Jack, and what's a lonely girl supposed to do? Pip seemed a 'safe option' I suppose - though that didn't stop me from having a couple of quick vodkas before he turned up.

"He was all puffed up when he arrived. It was quite funny. Told me steak was his speciality, and that he had a foolproof method for cooking it perfectly. I was amused - especially when, after about five minutes, it became perfectly clear that he was about to cremate the meat. Still, he rescued it well enough. I made all the right noises, then decided to cut to the chase. Half-an-hour later I discovered his approach to sex was exactly the same to cooking steak - though far less sophisticated: a minute-and-a-half, no turning over. Perhaps his dad had told him how to do that too. I ended up with my rump slightly warmed on one side and the meat cold in the middle!

"Well I wasn't having any of that! I think for a very short while I made his head spin - his head and a few other parts of his anatomy! But within a couple of weeks I knew there was no future with him. To be honest he just wasn't very interesting, and I'd started to socialise with some people I'd met at work, you know? Things were looking up - especially with Amir from accounts. So as I cut him loose, poor Pip just withered on the vine... It's been years since I last saw him - but he did teach me how to cook steak, I'll give him that."

Blue

It simply wasn't her colour. She'd known it all along. But with it being the last unopened bottle in the designer collection Mags had bought her for Christmas… Well, it had nagged at her for weeks, its protest growing increasingly loud. What was the point of having such a luxury if you weren't going to use it? Leaving it untouched felt a bit like betrayal; Mags had little enough money as it was, so for her to buy that large set as a present was saying something - copy-cat branding notwithstanding.

Having never been stressed since it left the factory (somewhere abroad, that's for sure, as it couldn't have been an English colour) it took her a while to loosen the stiff cap and remove the applicator from the fluid; doing so immediately confirmed it was not a shade for her. She had nothing against blue, of course. If you were to scan her wardrobe you'd find a few blue things: a long flouncy skirt which really suited her, but which she'd refused to wear since it had been overtaken by fashion; the ribbed jumper - nowadays a size too small - that accentuated *all* her curves and not merely those she would want to emphasise; the skimpy bikini which had landed her in a spot of bother when she had donned it on holiday in Magaluf that time… In spite of its somewhat checkered history however, the latter remained the kind of thing you still packed when you went on holiday - just in case you woke up one day in the mood to take a risk or two.

Once the lid was off the varnish she felt committed, so applied a thin coat of the liquid to the nail of the little finger of her left hand. Extending her arm, she looked at the freshly decorated digit from as great a distance as possible to see if doing so might alter her perception of the colour, to see if there was any chance the varnish would whisper - rather than shout - 'blue'. Having steeled herself to instantly remove the gloss when it proved too offensive, she was slightly surprised to find herself pushing on, glazing a second finger and then the final three in sequence until all on her left hand were decorated. She had blown on each in turn, then once again held her hand as far away as she could. "It's definitely blue", she said to herself, an air of resignation mixed with a sliver of surprise; she had never expected to get this far. Switching hands, she began the slightly slower process of varnishing her remaining fingers, doubly cautious because of the way the brush felt awkward in her left hand. Once finished, she placed the bottle on the table in front of her, replaced the applicator inside it, then extended both arms. There could be no doubt that it was very blue.

It was the sort of colour Mags would have worn in a heartbeat. More than that, it was highly unlikely she would have left it to be the last bottle opened. Bryony knew her well enough to understand that the seals on the most vibrant of pinks would have been broken first, then she would have focussed on the less conventional and more outrageous colours. She had more than one Goth-type look that demanded black fingernails, and several bold outfits which she would have endorsed with accents of bright yellow or vivacious green. It was not that she thought Mags excessively vain or shallow - though without doubt she possessed an above-average degree of both attributes, certainly sufficient for Bryony to take self-centred superficiality as her defining characteristic. First impressions and all that…

They had got off on the wrong foot in a conflict over a boy who, thanks to his repeated betrayals, was to eventually prove himself unworthy of both of them, their mutual hostility soon superseded by coming together as allies with a sharp focus on revenge and a somewhat manufactured plea for mutual support. For many, such a foundation might have proven rock-solid, but there was something about Mags which forced Bryony to keep a little of herself in reserve. Even after their separate affairs with Dom and the subsequent alliance, she felt she could only extend her trust so far. And although Mags had subsequently proven herself more than once, for some reason Bryony hadn't managed to resolve the question as to whether or not their partnership was destined to be long-term.

Over the next two years all evidence supported the theory that it was. They became - in common parlance - 'as thick as thieves', and were almost invariably seen together on a Saturday night in town, gracing The Matrix, Alfie's, or The Pyramid Rooms. As a duo they proved formidable enough for the male of the species; on more than one occasion, pairs of lounge-suited predators would try their luck only to be ruthlessly discarded once they had served their purpose. It was an approach they never chose to analyse. Was it a throwback to their experience with Dom, or were they simply a couple of young women looking out for each other while having fun? Not that there weren't the odd rocky moments. Mags had been with Bryony that time in Magaluf and, had the latter taken her advice in relation to one of the locals to whom Bryony had taken a shine… well, there would have been one less incident. Mags had bristled at not being listened too - and then bristled a little more when she found herself alone for a whole day thanks to her friend's impulsiveness. Being proved right hardly helped. But at least they had been mature enough to put it behind them, wordlessly resolving escapades bookended by flights out of and back into the UK by designating 'a holiday' as an acceptable excuse for many things. The manicure set had been Mags' present to her that Christmas. Even though she had been the one who had stepped out of line, Bryony came to think of the gift as an apology; it was a perspective that suited her.

Looking at her nails again - this time as her fingers went about the business of tidying up, putting things away - Bryony couldn't help but feel a little surprised that the nail varnish had triggered memory in such a way. And that it didn't seem to be the gift itself which had acted as the catalyst, but rather the colour. The blue flicked and flashed in front of her eyes as she stood up and went into the kitchen, as she put on the kettle, as she made coffee. For a moment she wondered if she hadn't made a mistake after all; whether, having tried it on that first finger, she shouldn't have returned to her original plan and simply wiped it away and progressed no further. But now it was too late - especially as she was already intrigued to find out what her colleagues were going to say when she turned up in the office to start the working week decorated in such a way. How long would it take for someone to put two and two together and made a joke about Blue Monday? Not that she had even been a New Order fan, of course. Nor of any band in particular, come to that; as long as the music got her to her feet. In some respects this ambivalence was how Bryony was about many things. She would only take adoption of a band, a brand, a style, so far; she had favourites, of course she did, but liked to believe such loyalties should never be beyond question. Perhaps her attraction to the fleeting - whether infatuations in Magaluf or the tolerance of blue nail varnish for the consequent prize of a one-off reaction from her workmates - was a reflection of that philosophy too. Maybe it was also partially responsible for how she now felt about Mags.

It wasn't that they had fallen out; falling out implies discord, conflicting points of view. There had been none of that. Being seen together as a duo at Saturday-night hotspots had begun to be superseded when Bryony found herself at The Pyramid Rooms as the third in a threesome. Mags had met Seb there some weeks previously and a relationship that had started as nothing out of the ordinary was soon promoted; what began as inconsequential had turned into something else. Three weeks after Mags first meeting him, Seb had still been around. More than that, circumstantial evidence - long phone calls, far-away looks, wistful silences when she and Mags were together - offered signs that her friend was in danger of moving on in a major way. More than once Bryony had called on her experience in Magaluf and tested her friend against that - and against their joint experience of Dom - to see if she could shake Mags from what she wanted to be nothing more than brief infatuation. But Mags seemed more committed than she had ever seen her - and being committed relegated Bryony to second place. When they first went to Alfie's as a threesome she had put in the hard yards to appear lively, engaged, cheerful, supportive. But it was clear soon after (if not that first evening) that she was in the way; she had shifted from being Mags' leading lady to little more than a bit-part player. It was a role in which she had no interest. For a while it had saddened her, and although she tried to maintain the charade of comradeship, she was conscious of doing it less and less well, and so risked becoming increasingly marginalised.

The previous evening - just a little over twelve hours earlier - she had decided to go to The Pyramid Rooms on her own. It had been a throwback to how it used to be. She had told herself it would be fine, if different. But that had been to ignore the fact that most of the men there - the ones who were on the hunt for young women out on their own - had not changed at all, and she found herself feeling uncomfortable, fending off unwanted attention, unable to dance as she wanted, as she would have with Mags. And then, as she contemplated an early retirement from the battlefield, she had seen Mags and Seb on the far side of the dance-floor. They hadn't even told her they were going.

She looked at her fingernails again and realised they were coated in a blue that reflected how she felt - and also, with the final bottle in the set having been opened, knowing she could now throw the whole lot away. Taking her coffee into the living room, she opened her laptop and headed for Expedia where she typed in 'Magaluf'. She'd already had enough of blue.

An Irregular Piece Of Sky

"Life," she said, "is a bit like peeling Brussels sprouts."

He had been sitting at the dining table worrying at a jigsaw puzzle with too much sky, her words coming through the hatch that separated him from the kitchen. Increasingly uniform blue shapes stared back at him defiantly. The space that remained to be filled openly challenged him.

"You start with a decent sized one, but then, by the time you've taken off the blemished leaves round the outside… Well, they're half the size."

From the timbre of her voice and the way it was slightly raised, he could tell she had assumed not only was he still sitting at the table but that he was also listening.

"And you can spice them up with tiny bits of bacon and whatnot, but in the end they're still sprouts."

As if in defiance of the puzzle, his fingers picked up a piece at random and, more by luck than judgement, instantly found its location. The small segment of sky fell into place with a satisfying 'snap', the result of slightly tensing the card to get the desired effect.

"How are you getting on?" she asked, prompted by the sound.

"What do you mean about sprouts and life?" he said, returning with his own question.

"Don't you mind me and my nonsense."

She smiled over her shoulder as if he could see her.

His eyes sought out another piece, a darker shade of blue with just a fragment of a wall intruding on one corner.

Sean had only been fourteen that day but thought he knew well enough what she meant about life being like peeling sprouts. As well a fourteen-year-old could, anyway. He now knew it was an age when, in reality, you didn't really know anything at all. You were a sponge, soaking up information and experience, trying to dissect and refine things, catalogue them, apply learnings to the world. Your education was all about trying to make sense of the kaleidoscope in which you lived, and because there was so much going on, so much to know and see and learn, most teenagers mistook being a sponge for gaining knowledge. But it wasn't knowledge at all. It was 'data'. And even though you could pretend to yourself that you were acquiring wisdom, in truth that only came later, once you'd harvested it through living your own life and making your own mistakes. Only then did things start making sense. There needed to be a catalyst to turn 'data' into true knowledge.

Back then his belief that he understood what his mother meant by her sprouts comment was based on recognising some of the influences behind it, primarily the reality of their shared life together and their divergent experiences of his father. It was only now - years later - he realised he had been subsuming those things through the protective filter of a shallow veneer; he had not 'lived' them in the same way as she had. Her perspective was entirely different, as was her starting point. The fact that new and uncontrollable hormones were then raging through his body did nothing to aid understanding, even if he naïvely interpreted them as helping. Not that Sean suffered from the wildness many teenage boys embraced; if he had, he wouldn't have been sitting at the dining room table trying to fill a sky-shaped hole in a thousand-piece jigsaw. He would have been in town with his friends, trying out cigarettes or Special Brew, and then chewing spearmint gum to mask the smell; he would have been hanging around the park with Chrissie and her friends, trying to 'big himself up', to make out he was already man enough to accept the favours she was rumoured to dispense on a Saturday evening despite her relatively tender age. But that was probably more fantasy than reality too - even if he'd been unable to see it. The Chrissie he'd known in the Fourth Form was, after all, just a hormonal cauldron too.

It had become a regular weekend scene, Sean at a jigsaw on the dining room table, his Mother busy in the kitchen either indulging in her vaguely experimental cooking or with the ironing board up. One way or another it had been like this on a Saturday afternoon for a while, even when his Father had still been around. Their routine began in the morning when she would go into town to do the shopping and Sean would locate himself in the section of the table free from jigsaw pieces in order to do his homework. She used to describe their respective endeavours as their 'chores'. "Saturday afternoon and all the chores done!" she would say. It was as if they had freed themselves, in theory allowing the remainder of the weekend to be opened up to all sorts of adventures. That she did so with little regard for any plans his father might have had served them well for the time when he was no longer around to be considered at all.

Sean became adept at getting through his homework in the two-hour window set aside expressly for the purpose. Occasionally, when he didn't have enough official school work to fill the time, he would supplement it with extra reading, or perhaps a secondary effort at something which required him to be creative. Very occasionally he had no homework at all - usually at the beginning or end of term - and so they would go into town shopping together, an event invariably marked by scones at Baxter's.

On the day of his Mother's comment about life and sprouts, he'd had Maths, Chemistry and English, and tackled them in that order - the things he found easiest first. When she had said "life is a bit like peeling Brussels sprouts" he'd just given up on the opening scenes of *Macbeth* for the umpteenth time. For the previous hour or so he had read and re-read, took the notes he thought he was supposed to take, and tried to remember how the whole story played out. He was diligent, if nothing else. He tried to imagine being Macbeth or one of the witches to see if that helped him understand what was really going on, but he didn't have the imagination for it. Finishing partially defeated, he had turned to his puzzle a little earlier than usual.

Although their weekend routine must have been different at some point, it seemed to Sean as if it had always been the same. The fact that two years earlier he had been in a different school - and before that there had been three of them sitting down to breakfast - did nothing to dispel his sense that it had been ever thus. Perhaps that feeling was a byproduct of the stability his mother offered him.

To be fair however, it was probably more than that. That morning - his mind having not yet fully flushed through the residue of his English homework - Sean tried to think of attributes he could apply to her in addition to 'stability'. Constancy came first to mind. She had always been there for him - even when things were difficult. And she was consistent too, even though Sean knew maintaining consistency would, at times, have been supremely hard. She liked order and routine - their Saturday mornings were evidence enough of that! - and this struck a chord with him, the joy of not needing to think about 'what to do next' because it was worked out in advance, understood, perfected. There was something comforting knowing they would end up in Baxter's whenever they went into town together. This was small scale fortune-telling however. Whether she could foresee it or not, Sean knew she disliked change, especially big, complicated and messy change, and although she never said anything outright, he was sure that she too liked the structure of their weekends as demonstrated by "Saturday afternoon and all the chores done!" Stability, constancy, consistency; traits that would gradually bleed from her in the years which followed.

Perhaps those attributes were the influences leading to the comment about Brussels sprouts and the disappointment inherent in vegetable peeling. Even though her remark had been a practical complaint - as well as encompassing a lot of other things a fourteen year-old couldn't possibly appreciate - he wondered if there might be some relief in it too. If sprouts were always thus, wasn't that a 'good thing'? What would happen if, one morning, she suddenly didn't need to peel away the outer leaves, or if nearly a hundred percent remained to be cooked at the end of a much abbreviated process? How unsettling would that be for her?

Over the next four years or so, their lives changed very little, though that wasn't to say things weren't different. How could they not be as Sean tried to navigate puberty on his journey to manhood? If he chose to think about it now, he could recall a few incidents of disharmony and conflict alongside the various elements of growing-up that actually proved more problematic: mainly, but not exclusively, in how he should relate to girls. In more than one area - and across multiple incidents - when faced with an inability to work out exactly what was going on, he would retreat into landscapes where he felt most comfortable. He sensed that his mother sometimes felt as if he was actually failing to grow up at all. Occasionally she would chastise him for not being more outgoing, more adventurous. Why wasn't he out with his friends on a Saturday evening? Why didn't he go to parties or discos, or be bad and stay out until two in the morning so that she could chastise him? On more than one occasion she had tried to tempt him with drink and cigarettes - two vices playing an increasingly prominent role in her own life, though at that stage Sean never really understood why. And then there had been that particularly black Sunday morning when, in a uniquely foul temper, she had swept a three-quarter finished jigsaw from the dining table and onto the floor. She had been instantly contrite, but Sean did not forgive her - nor speak to her - until he had salvaged all the pieces and, three days later, completed the puzzle. It had been excruciating for both of them.

In spite of such rare clashes, the core of their lives remained the same. While he was struggling with the hormone overdose nature had gifted him - as well as impending examinations and the looming prospect of University - not having to worry about the mechanics of 'living' was to be welcomed. He believed it suited her too, especially if he ignored her gradually increasing reliance on alcohol. His assumption that it was either 'a phase' or 'an age thing' allowed him to brush it under the carpet.

He was increasingly worried about leaving her, though. It was a dread which crept up on him with stealth, punctuated by unavoidable milestones relating to his education. As soon as his path into the Sixth Form had been confirmed via decent if not spectacular exam grades, teachers in general - and his mother in particular - forced him to recognise that he would, without question, be going on to university and therefore needed to think about the course he would want to take. For a while he contributed passively to conversations on the subject - until deadlines for applications began to loom and he knew he could absent himself no longer.

"You are not staying in this God-forsaken town!" she had said decisively over dinner one evening about a week before his UCAS forms were due in, this being her somewhat explosive response to his proposal that he submit a single application to the local college. She would have none of it and, she argued, his school would surely take a dim view of such a limp proposal. 'Limp' had been her word. Sean knew she was right but felt unable to confess that his notion of not moving away was not to suit him but rather because he was concerned about *her*, about the impact of his change, how well she might cope by being on her own. His was a silence due only in part to a lack of moral courage. Against her theory that he needed to leave home in order to learn how to become independent and thus finish the process of growing up - a theory she advocated eloquently and vehemently - he came to realise that any objection would be trivialised and then trampled underfoot, no matter how well-intentioned their secret origins. So he chose and ranked five universities, none more than three hours away by public transport. Given he didn't really care where he went or what he studied (in the end History seemed a safe enough bet) his final choice of locations offered a suitable compromise. Once his form had been submitted and the topic taken off the table, associated flash-points dissolved away too. Sean believed that for a while she even eased back a little on the drinking. It felt like a victory, though he was not entirely sure for who.

In all probability his mother's decline did not accelerate when he had left home, but given he next saw her some seven weeks after his departure, a number of subtle changes had accumulated in such a way that he encountered them as a single larger package; perhaps the whole greater than the sum of the parts. Like everyone else during those initial University weeks, he had been swept along with the newness of everything: the course, his tutors, the new friends he was making. It felt like starting not just a new chapter, but a whole new life. There were rules to learn - written or otherwise - and in the beginning elements from his past upon which he had relied (and taken for granted!) occasionally tripped him up with their absence. Saturday morning sessions of homework and jigsaw were replaced by sleeping in later, casual breakfasts, even the odd hangover. Excursions to Baxter's were things of the past, superseded by loosely coordinated trips to the supermarket when he and two or three of his flatmates would pile into a less-than-reliable Astra and invade the nearby Sainsbury's. New routines expanded, stealthily embellishing the embryonic scaffolding provided by his course timetable.

If he was surprised to notice the change in his mother that first weekend back, what *she* must have felt in seeing *him* would have been off the scale. "Look at you!" she had said when he crossed the threshold, somehow unable to take him all in at once. The myriad of questions which followed allowed her to piece together an image of Sean's new life, but it was impressionistic at best, fragmented owing to his inability to convey exactly what it felt like to be out in the world on his own - that old failing of the creative in him! Perhaps his new-found sense of independence, of learning to be his own man, forced him to see his mother in a new light too. He remarked, as if for the first time, things which had always been there and were now more visible: the frequency of her smoking, now at least two cigarettes an hour; the glasses of sherry she found occasion to excuse over lunch or as she cooked; the change in the ratio between the gin and the tonic at dinner. That Saturday afternoon, when helping sort out the recycling, he could only be struck by the number of empty bottles which would be awaiting collection that coming Monday. His questions for her were batted away as if they were irrelevant. Drawing a parallel with his own reinvention, he asked her what she had been doing with her time, certain that his not being there would have freed up much of it. That went unanswered too.

"Why don't we go to Baxter's?"

It was a suggestion made through the serving hatch as he stood in the dining room mid-afternoon, his eyes wandering over the naked dining table, the sounds of his mother washing-up leaking through from the kitchen.

"What was that?"

"Baxter's. Why don't we go? My treat."

She laughed as if it had been the most ridiculous idea she had ever heard, and came smiling to the small window that stood open between them.

"I don't think so, Dear. Why would I want to share you with anyone else?"

He smiled dutifully.

"When do you need to be getting back?"

"I should leave tomorrow afternoon; after lunch. I have an early lecture on Monday. Actually, Monday's my one pretty heavy day."

She shook her head, still smiling.

"Listen to him! Monday lectures, indeed! Well then."

It was as if the answer had defeated his own proposition, the consequence of which was an afternoon spent largely in front of the television except for half an hour where he excused himself to go for a short walk 'round the block'. "Your old stomping ground" she said, as if he'd ever had such a thing.

"There's something you need to know about your father." Her words came out of the blue when they were settled down to watch the obligatory Saturday-evening gameshow. This too had been part of their shared weekend ritual, but the one which Sean now realised he missed least of all.

He looked at his mother. Although the first commercial break had just intruded into the show - and perhaps in consequence had acted as the opportunity for her statement - her eyes remained resolutely fixed on the television.

"I could have told you some time ago," she carried on, superficially intent on an advert for hair colouring, "but there didn't seem to be a right time. And now that you're away and getting so grown-up - well, I've no excuse any more."

"Dad?"

"About before he left." She paused to allow Sean to establish and fix a point in time. He had been eleven or so the day she announced that from then on it was going to be just the two of them against the world. "And a little bit about me too, I suppose."

He didn't know what to say. It felt inappropriate to prompt, so he simply waited until she was ready. A trio of long-haired beauties - blonde, brunette and redhead - flounced up to the camera and pursed their lips in an exaggerated kiss.

"When you were - what? - seven I suppose. I fell pregnant. Your father and I had already agreed that we weren't going to have any more children; your arrival had been hard enough, for me at least!" She laughed, now looking his way to try and assure him that she was partly joking. "There were lots of late night conversations about what we should do, about risks and rewards. In the end, we decided we should try and see if we could give you a brother or sister."

Sean couldn't miss something in the tone which seemed to suggest an abdicated decision, laying the responsibility for their choice on what they thought *he* might need. He said nothing.

"For a very short while everything was fine, but then I got sick. My body. It simply wasn't up to a second child." She paused, glanced back to the television when the quiz show's theme tune announced the end of the adverts. "So the decision was taken out of our hands. I had to have a termination. You might remember I went away for a few days? We concocted some story about your grandparents I think. Anyway…"

On the television, the gameshow's host gleamed at some new contestants who had just been introduced, slipping seamlessly into his standard patter. Sean tried to think back to when he was seven to see if he could dredge up a memory of his mother not being there.

"It broke us." Her words drew him back from both the television and his memories. "Me physically, of course. After what I went through - and what they did to me - there were never going to be any more second chances."

"And Dad?"

"Your father? He took it much harder than I'd expected. It might surprise you to know that of the two of us he was always the keen one. Unlike me, he'd grown up in a big family, of course. Oh, he disguised his disappointment well enough at first; very caring and attentive, that kind of thing. But soon it was clear there was now something new between us. I suppose, he thought I was to blame for not being able to honour my side of the deal." She paused and looked vaguely around the room as if to see whether there was something else she should be doing rather than unburden herself of her history. Finding nothing, she pushed on. "Slowly he became - I don't know - distant, I suppose. And then he started..." Here the pause became exaggerated, as if she couldn't find the words - or having indeed located them, was aware they had become lodged somewhere on the journey from her heart to her mouth. "He started to see other women."

"He had an affair?"

She laughed. It was a soft, resigned sound, bereft of any joy.

"Affairs. Plural. Maybe he couldn't help himself. Maybe it was me. I don't know. He tried to keep his dalliances secret - because that's all they were in the beginning, dalliances. But I knew; I could tell. And I let him carry on. For maybe two years or so. I didn't challenge him or accuse him; the most important thing at that point became you. I wanted to keep us together for as long as I could..."

Sean felt his burden growing.

"But in the end that was taken out of my hands too. One day a dalliance turned into something more serious, and a year later your father left. That was it. All over. It was just you and me."

A burst of applause assaulted them from the television. Sean knew from past experience it was the sound of consolation, bestowed on a couple who have just missed out on the jackpot.

"Did you ever guess?" She delivered this as if it were the most important question of all, the one that would define whether or not she had been successful in protecting him.

He felt an incalculable weight attach itself to his answer. How could he respond adequately?

"About?" He stalled.

"Any of it. All of it."

'All of it' seemed such a vast concept, something which encapsulated not just his father's infidelities and abandonment of them, but his mother's frailties and failures too. 'All of it' spoke to a lifetime of collective inadequacies. Like a Black Hole, it drew into itself everything from his universe. He imagined himself as he would have been years earlier, sitting in the dining room, mesmerised as the pieces of his jigsaw levitated from the table, sucked into an invisible vortex. Through the kitchen hatch came the sounds of her voice, the scraps from her vegetable peelings, all being whisked up, blended into everything else until nothing remained distinct, the world a whorl of fragments and noise. And what seemed like moments later - though stretched across a desert of years - Sean saw himself there again, as he had been just a few hours ago, staring at that self same table and wondering where all those irregular blue jigsaw pieces had gone.

"No," he said, "I never guessed."

And even though he saw some of the tension leave her body as if his answer had unburdened her, Sean knew he should try and elaborate. It was more than not guessing. It was not seeing, not understanding, not comprehending; it was about being ignorant and innocent; about the sudden recognition that, as a child, he had aligned himself to a set of rules, processes and beliefs that were now proven to be no more than vapour. Clicking piece after piece of jigsaw in place to solve a void of sky was meaningless, self-deluding; it represented nothing in terms of achievement, a fact that no-one - not even his mother - had ever divulged. And more than all of that, there was now the question as to why the world worked that way, and why those things he had previously used to navigate through his life were ultimately worthless. Hadn't his father's betrayal proved that? Weren't the smoking and drinking merely manifestations of her own recognition - conscious or otherwise - of the emptiness of it all? As he looked at her - focussed once more on the television - Sean wondered if she had been trying to give him clues all along, as if, even now, the extra-strong gins were code for something else. Had she too looked into the abyss and watched her world being sucked away?

From somewhere a memory surfaced. Perhaps this was a message too, but one he realised he never had understood until now.

"Life," he said, "is a bit like peeling Brussels sprouts."

"What's that?" She turned her head to look at him, her face quizzical, suggesting she had misheard.

"Nothing," he said, trying a smile. "It doesn't matter."

Acknowledgements

Previous publications:

- "After All This Time" first appeared in *Marking Marks in the Sand*, Coverstory books, 2022.

- "Park'n'Ride" first appeared in *New Contexts: 3*, Coverstory books, 2022, and won First Prize in the Writers' Summer School, Swanwick 2022, short story prize.

www.ingramcontent.com/pod-product-compliance
Lightning Source LLC
Chambersburg PA
CBHW070351200726
48294CB00003B/839